THE HOUNDS OF DEVOTION

EVA CHASE

The Hounds of Devotion

Book 3 in the Moriarty's Men series

First Digital Edition, 2019

Copyright © 2019 Eva Chase

Cover design: Deranged Doctor Design

Ebook ISBN: 978-1-989096-40-6

Paperback ISBN: 978-1-989096-41-3

 Created with Vellum

CHAPTER ONE

Jemma

Throughout my career, from when I'd first struck out on my own at fourteen years old and started carving a space for myself, officers of the law had been people to avoid or overcome. I certainly never expected to find myself sitting at a table with three of the most esteemed crime-fighters in the world, all of them aiming to help me.

Garrett Lestrade took a swig from his beer and motioned to the tablet he'd set on the table, looking perfectly at home even though the apartment belonged to his two colleagues. I'd gathered that Scotland Yard's youngest detective inspector had joined Sherlock and John for many a dinner over the last few years. Despite being only a smidge taller than me and wiry in frame, the intensity in his pose and boyish face gave him just as much presence as the other two.

"Looking for similar patterns of crimes to what we saw when locating the commune in Croatia, I'd say that cult of yours has some sort of base over here in the Lake District."

He motioned to the map he'd brought up on the tablet's screen. "Somewhere along the outskirts, I'd assume, away from the popular hiking paths. They do seem to like their mountainous areas, don't they?"

"They do." I leaned forward to consider the spot he'd indicated and took another bite from the cinnamon cookie I'd been nibbling on, which was the best dessert I'd been able to scrounge up here. Sherlock and John had a disturbing lack of sweets in their apartment. "The shrouded folk draw on the sun for energy, and the higher the elevation, the more they can absorb."

The corner of Garrett's mouth twitched downward at the comment, just for a second. My trio of criminal investigators was only starting to fully wrap their heads around the idea that a sort of demonic faerie creatures existed and spread their malicious influence through our world. It was easy enough for me to believe, having grown up with the monsters.

The thought of those early childhood rituals, swaying in the sun while drawing lines of blood into my skin with a tiny blade, sent a cold shudder through me that I held tightly inside.

Sherlock Holmes, both the most skeptical and the keenest thinker among the trio, tapped his narrow chin with a distant expression as if absorbing that fact for later analysis. He took a puff from his pipe, thickening the earthy smoky smell in the air, and tugged the tablet closer. "Would we assume the cult has only *one* base of operations in all of England? You gave the impression they were rather more widespread than that, Jemma."

"There might be others," Garrett said quickly. "That was only the spot with the clearest pattern. I have other possibilities as well, but we decided we'd start with the most likely, didn't we?"

Sherlock regarded him evenly, his pale blue eyes sharp beneath the messy fall of his wavy dark brown hair. As well as they worked together, I'd had many opportunities to observe the tension that existed between the two men, Garrett always striving to prove himself just as adept as the brilliant and widely lauded Sherlock.

"I find it best to have all the potential threads at my disposal," the consulting detective said.

As so often, it was John Watson who eased that tension, with all the warmth he must have brought to his medical practice before his stint in the army had brought that career to an end. He shook his blond head ruefully. "I'm sure Garrett can go over all the patterns he found in the police records later. The location he named does match up with our suspicions from our own investigations. Why don't we focus on our next steps for now?"

"Yes," I said, with a drumming of my fingers on the table's edge. I wasn't used to collaborating with so many people directly. While our alliance was clearly working to my benefit—the trio had access to resources it'd be much harder for me to get my hands on—I couldn't say the extended back-and-forth felt exactly comfortable. "We can only tackle one of these communes at a time. And while I'd be surprised if there weren't at least two or three in the whole of this country, whichever one's showing the most obvious markers ought to be the largest and the one it's most important to take down."

The other man at the table, the one who'd always been on my side, lifted his jaw toward me. He spoke low and firm. "This is Jemma's operation. We go by what she says."

Sebastian Moran knew how to cut to the chase. The

hitman who'd become my right-hand man—and closest confidant, and recently lover—also exuded power with his presence. Just a few weeks ago, he'd been perfectly ready to shoot all three of our London trio rather than debate with them to save my life. A fact I doubted any of the three would soon forget. His brawny arms flexed as he shifted in his seat as if to provide an additional reminder.

Most of Bash was dark, from the stubble of black hair on his tan scalp to the glower he could turn on in an instant, but a spark of admiration lit in his light green eyes as he fixed his gaze on me.

"How can we best go about taking down these monsters?" he said. "It's not like Croatia—you were mostly looking to get that knife from the commune there."

"Although it was a welcome addition that our strategy meant the arrest of most of the cult members as well." I exhaled slowly. I'd had years to plan for this moment, but I'd planned for going it alone. In the last several days, as the men around me had begun their investigations and I'd recuperated from the ceremony that had freed me from my deal with one of the shrouded folk, I'd had plenty of time to think about other approaches that would better utilize the keenness now at my disposal.

"I actually think that the approach we used before might be adapted quite well to other circumstances," I went on. "The short of it is, I want the shrouded folk cut off from this world. Let them skulk around in their own realm, wherever that may be, so no person here ever has a reason to offer up the bloody sacrifices they demand. And it's the people in those communes, making those sacrifices, who open the doorway for the shrouded folk to come here."

Sherlock nodded, understanding sparking in his eyes. He might still find it hard to believe in my supernatural beasts, but he could follow a chain of logic nonetheless. "If you can eliminate their avenues of support, you eliminate their access. We need to prevent these people from conducting the rituals that give these... things their power."

"Exactly." I shot him a smile as a little thrill tingled through me. Perhaps there was something strange about this man devoted to dealing out justice allying himself with a consummate criminal, but I couldn't help enjoying the sharpness of his wits. Sherlock was the only man who'd ever gotten the better of me, if merely temporarily. The challenge had been exhilarating, and having him put those skills to work on my behalf might have been even more so.

"And root out their accursed line," Bash murmured with a dark smile of his own. Even though he often mocked the Shakespearean dramas he liked to watch, they stuck with him well enough to give him quotes at the ready.

"If all goes well," I said. "I think we need to be clear on one thing. These cultists—the ones who are adults, anyway—are hardly victims. They know full well the horrors the shrouded folk require, and they go along with them in exchange for existing near beings with that much unearthly power. Frankly, if I could simply have them all slaughtered and eliminate the folk's basis of support that way, I wouldn't see any problem with that."

John turned a bit green. "Well, I mean, they *are* people, even if they've been swayed by—"

I waved off his protest. "Don't worry. I'm not saying we slaughter them all. I just wanted to make the point that we can't let *ourselves* be swayed by misguided pity. Every person in those cults has been an accomplice to murder and has carried out torture, often of children. Keep that in mind when we're tackling this problem."

The doctor's mouth tightened. I could tell from the resolve in his expression that it wasn't my behavior he was objecting to the thought of now. I did enjoy John's softer side, especially when I got to experience it in intimate fashion, but I appreciated the strength he could summon underneath it just as much.

Bash chuckled. "If slaughter's off the table—more's the pity—you're thinking we sic the cops on them, Mori?"

"They *are* criminals, all of them," I said. "There'll be evidence of those crimes in every commune if we can justify a search like we did in Croatia. The cultists won't be able to conduct their rituals from a jail cell. But we need to arrange our police raids so they come by surprise, sweeping through swiftly and effectively."

"Any cult members who escape the sweep could go on with their practices elsewhere," Garrett filled in. He might not have quite the crystalline brilliance Sherlock possessed, but he was sharp in his own right—and full of a delicious passionate determination as well. "We cracked down on them easily before, and we've got better contacts and more clout here. We just need an urgent justification, like that kidnapping story we came up with."

Sherlock frowned. "As well as that gambit worked, we can't simply go around conjuring false crimes if we're going to be tackling several of these communes. Our credibility will take a beating before we're even a fraction of the way through this mission."

"I agree." I might not have any need to worry about my own credibility with the police—we wouldn't get into how many times I'd pulled the wool over their eyes or misdirected them before—but my trio of detectives wouldn't be much use to me if they lost their standing. "But the cult commits plenty of real crimes. We'll need to set them up for an illicit act where we're pulling the strings, and then we can tip off the local cops."

"Presumably we're not going to set up a murder," John said.

I patted his arm. "Don't you worry about that either, my dear doctor," I said teasingly. "They've got a perfect weakness for us to exploit that doesn't involve any blood spilled at all."

"Their penchant for theft," Sherlock said.

"There you have it." A sly grin curled my lips. "In particular, the communes always need medical supplies to offset their bloodletting and other horrific rituals. They can hardly bring a sliced-up child into a hospital without provoking an instant investigation. So we'll dangle a jackpot they can't resist: a large shipment of antibiotics and other essentials that'd last them for years. We don't even need an actual shipment—they just need to believe we have one."

Bash straightened up. "I assume that's where I come in."

My gut pinched with a hint of guilt as I shook my head. Normally, spreading any kind of public information would have been my hitman's job, while I orchestrated events in the background. But I had to take full advantage of all my allies' strengths.

"I may want you in there later," I said. "But Sherlock and John know their way around a disguise and can play off each other well. Better to start spreading the word with conversations simply overhead rather than making any direct inquiries."

John's eyes gleamed with the prospect of getting down to work. "I'd imagine we could arrange to be overheard all over the Lake District."

"What do you need on the official side of things?" Garrett asked, his stance tensed as if he was afraid I wasn't going to need him at all.

I caressed his hand reassuringly, a flicker of heat racing through me at the desire that simple touch could light in his eyes. Garrett could be passionate about all sorts of things, but I loved it most when he aimed that passion at me.

"You'll have plenty to keep you busy," I said. "I think we should start spreading the word about the cult within law enforcement circles. The news isn't likely to have traveled all the way from Croatia, but you've got a perfectly good reason to talk about it, since you were there. If everyone is primed for a cult full of horrors, we'll be able to push them into action faster."

He tipped his head to me, looking satisfied.

I turned to Bash. "You and I are going to do some covert scouting out around the Lake District to see if we can't narrow down the commune's location."

Bash gave me his slow smile. "I'm up for that." He paused. "How careful do you need to be around these things? You broke whatever contract you had with that one, but some of them would recognize you, wouldn't they?"

"Maybe. I don't know exactly how they move around our world, whether all of them draw on all the communes or whether they stick mainly to certain locations." I rubbed my mouth. "Most of my association with them happened in the United States. But those ones may have a presence here too—and the one I had the contract with may have spread a general warning."

The shrouded folk had rules about impinging on the natives of this world. They wanted to keep their presence reasonably secret from those unaware of them. But they already knew *I* was aware of them. If they caught me in isolation, I wouldn't put it past them to attempt to kill me. They'd already done that once just after I'd severed the contract.

Sherlock got up from the table. "I might have something that can help with that concern."

He ducked into his bedroom and emerged holding four gleaming gold pieces etched with mathematical patterns and embedded with tiny gems. A laugh tumbled from my lips.

"You picked it up during that dash for your lives."

He shrugged with his usual confidence. "It seemed the sort of thing that might come in handy again."

It certainly was. Those gold pieces could connect together into a cuff that prevented the shrouded folk from detecting a person. It'd kept me hidden from the fiend that wanted to claim my soul for weeks until I'd been able to free myself from that contract.

Bash's forehead furrowed. "That relic made you sick when you were wearing it before."

"Only after I'd had it on much longer than it was ever intended to be used for. I'm back to full health now. I can't imagine it'll hurt to wear it for a few hours here and there while we get the lay of the land." I accepted the gold pieces from Sherlock and raised an eyebrow at him. "I trust there won't be any trouble over the acquiring of the one piece?"

I'd stolen the final piece I needed from under the trio's noses—and with their unwitting help—months ago.

The corner of Sherlock's mouth quirked upward. "I find I can overlook the theft of an item stolen from a long-time thief and miscreant."

"All right then." My fingers closed around the smooth metal. My gaze slid over the men assembled around me, and a quiver of excitement raced through my chest. "Let's destroy those bastards."

CHAPTER TWO

John

Our fifth pub of the day was the kind of place I'd call "colorful" if I was being generous. In a less optimistic mood, I'd probably have gone with "sleazy." The lights were dim, the booths shadowy, the tables a hotchpotch of garish reds and oranges. The tang of alcohol hung in the air so thick you could practically get tipsy simply by breathing, and from the raucous laughter that pealed out every few seconds, everyone in here other than Sherlock and me was already at least that drunk.

The laughter mixed with the lively rock song that was playing, which meant our voices weren't going to carry far. We'd picked a table close to a couple of booths full of the people Sherlock had deemed most likely to be criminal types through his various methods of deduction.

"We'll get the whole truck," he said to me in an affected accent, pitching his voice loud enough to rise over the music but not so loud it'd sound as if he meant to be overhead. "The driver's ready to step back and let us at it without raising a fuss. As long as he can claim robbery and get a small cut for his trouble, it's all ours."

"How much do you figure we can make off that kind of medical stuff?" I replied, doing my best to match his tone in my own altered voice.

"Ah, there's always need for antibiotics and the like. We'll make a good profit, don't you worry."

"Have you got a buyer lined up already? I don't want to try to be selling this load bit by bit. We'll need someone eager for the whole thing."

Sherlock shrugged with a grin that showed all his enjoyment at getting to put on a performance like this. We'd both donned disguises for this bit of subterfuge, but while most of his face was hidden behind a false beard and makeup, his light blue eyes remained the same. When they gleamed as brightly as they were right now, I found it hard to look away.

"I know how it goes," he said. "I'm sure I can find someone quickly enough. We'll have plenty of room to be flexible with the price and still have it be worth our while."

I couldn't tell if any of the blokes sitting in the booths were paying attention to our conversation, but reading people wasn't my specialty. Sherlock shifted back in his chair, giving every sign of satisfaction. If our gambit was going to land with anyone here, I supposed we'd said enough.

I edged my chair a tad closer to Sherlock's so we could talk without being overhead now. He reached for his whisky, neat, at the same time as I reached for my beer, and our elbows brushed against each other.

A few weeks ago, the jolt of electricity that shot through my nerves at the contact would have set me off-kilter. A few months before that, I'd have denied it even existed. Somehow or other, with her wiles and her all-too-perceptive gaze, Jemma had changed that.

Yes, I found the man in front of me as immensely attractive as he could be incredibly infuriating. Yes, I had acted on that attraction not just once but twice now. The first time might have been a disaster, but the second…

The memory of our mouths colliding sent another jolt straight to my groin. Sherlock hadn't run away that time. He'd met me halfway, and afterward he'd found it in him to admit he'd liked it, as awkwardly as he might have gotten that across.

Having any sort of relationship, even platonic, with my roommate, best friend, and colleague had never been simple. I'd intertwined my life with his knowing that, and I hadn't regretted it once. Now there was one more dimension to our partnership. So what if I'd never been attracted to any man other than him, and he'd never seemed much attracted to *anyone* before we encountered Jemma Moriarty? Navigating this new dimension might be awkward, but the feelings themselves were perfectly straightforward.

I took a gulp of my beer, an ale with a lot less body than I'd been able to get in the last pub. "I still find it hard to believe that Jemma's 'folk' influenced so many people without you catching on that there was something wrong. Do you think they're really as widespread as she suggests?"

Sherlock raised his shoulders again, but this time there was a hint of stiffness to his shrug. "I expect with her experience she'd be a much better judge of the particulars than we are. I've certainly known that various supernaturally focused cults exist. It simply never would have entered my mind that the supernatural aspect of their worship had any basis in reality."

"It's not just the supernatural, though, but the intersection with the real world. The thefts, the torture, the killings…"

"From what she's said, the sacrifices usually are made by the cult's own people. When they live so far apart from society, there's no way for any official body to keep track of possible crimes. They hardly pilfer enough medical supplies and the like to draw national, let alone international attention."

"No, I suppose that would go against their need for secrecy." I let out a wry laugh. "Even having seen them—having witnessed their attack on us and Jemma—it's hard to wrap my head around the fact that these things *do* exist. You don't think we could have—"

"I'm quite sure there is a ponderance of evidence in support of the creatures being real—I would never have so much as entertained the idea otherwise," Sherlock cut in, his normally smooth tenor going sharp.

I blinked at him. It wasn't like Sherlock to lose even a little of his temper—certainly not in the middle of a calm conversation with *me* of all people. Which meant, knowing him, it wasn't me or the conversation he was really irritated about.

"Do you think there's a factor we haven't considered that could become a problem?" I asked. "Or is this whole endeavor taking too much time away from your usual cases?"

Sherlock's stance had relaxed again. He turned his sweating glass between his slender fingers. "Oh, no. I suspect this will be the greatest case of my entire career, even if it'll also be the most secretive. Onward we go, and we'll deal with any unexpected factors as they arrive. It's an adventure, isn't it?"

I wasn't sure I totally believed the smile he aimed at me, but there was no point in pushing a subject if Sherlock had decided he didn't want to talk about it. He could lock himself up as tight as a bank vault.

I was reaching for a change of subject with a burly guy with a yellow bandana tied around his head jerked out the other chair at our small table, spun it around, and dropped into it with a decisive thump. He crossed his arms over the back and gave us a narrow stare. My pulse immediately kicked up a notch with a rush of adrenaline.

"You don't look like much for a couple of guys who talk a blue streak," the new arrival said in a growl of a voice. "But obviously you don't have much smarts twice over."

"I'm not sure I understand your meaning," Sherlock said evenly. "Care to explain?"

The tough guy counted off his point points on his meaty fingers. "First, you come in here blathering about your plans so's half the place knows about it already. Second, you didn't bother to ask around before you started nosing around here with your schemes. This territory is covered. Any deals you want to make, they go through my boss. Any deals you've already made, we take double for the disrespect."

I reached for my walking stick instinctively where I'd leaned it against the side of the table. The cool firm surface against my fingers solidified my confidence. The thump of my pulse propelled the words from my throat.

"I don't think you can lay dibs on a whole area like that. We'll talk about what we want where we want, and we'll make our deals without any payoffs."

The man focused his dark glower completely on me. His gaze slid to the stick for a second, and his lip curled with a sneer. He had no idea that I could use that tool as effectively in a skirmish as any weapon he might be carrying on him.

"I don't think you want to be picking fights you can't see through," he said.

Another burst of adrenaline flooded my veins. In that instant, I could taste how good it would feel to take this jerk on, to flex the combat muscles I rarely got to use, to see the shock on his face when I toppled him. It'd teach him a lesson about judging by appearances, and it'd give an extra gossip factor to help our story spread. I started to shift my weight onto my feet—

—and Sherlock set a hand on my thigh under the table, warning me to stay in place.

"We're not looking for any fight," he said, holding up his other hand in a gesture of submission. "No deals have been made yet. If you object to them happening around here, I'm sure we can take our business elsewhere."

The man scowled at him. "You'd better keep your partner in line. And if you're going to be messing around in these parts, you ask after Mick first. Got it?"

"Absolutely. I'm sorry for the confusion. In fact, I'd imagine we should be on our way now."

He let go of my leg and stood up, and there was nothing for me to do but follow him.

I started to reach for my glass to toss back the rest of my beer but decided the mediocre stuff wasn't worth it. Hefting my walking stick, I let it rap hard against the wooden floor just for the pleasure of watching the guy's muscles twitch. Then I stalked out of the pub after Sherlock, walking slowly so I could keep my pace perfectly even despite the twinge of my war injury in my hip. I'd rather the thug never realized I needed the stick for anything other than an affectation.

Sherlock headed straight to the car. Without any discussion, he got in on the passenger side, leaving the driving to me. I sank into the seat, but I didn't turn on the engine right away.

"I could have handled him," I felt the need to say.

"Of course you could have," Sherlock said. "But that's not what we're here for. A bar brawl hardly seems like the type of behavior that would enamor us to a group aiming to keep as low a profile as possible. We're looking to spread the word, not bruises."

I hadn't thought about that angle. A prickle of shame ran through me. "Right. Of course. I must have gotten a little too caught up in playacting the crook."

Sherlock chuckled. "Well, now you can work out some of that aggression by tackling the road with much vehemence, as you're so fond of doing." He consulted the map on his phone in the waning evening light. "I think we can manage one more stop before we turn in for the day. Do you figure you can cover fifty miles in half an hour?"

A different sort of thrill tingled through me. "You'd better believe it. Just remember that I haven't gotten us into an accident yet." In the grip of a sudden impulse, I leaned across the seats and planted a quick kiss on his lips. The feel of them, warm and dry and instinctively pressing back against mine, melted the last of my agitation.

When I pulled back, Sherlock blinked at me, startled but with a faint flush to his cheeks that didn't look displeased. "What was that about?" he said mildly.

"To clear our heads?" I suggested. That was the excuse Sherlock most often turned to when he allowed himself to indulge in sexual pleasure. The thought of all the ways

Jemma had heightened that pleasure made me momentarily giddy. I knew better than to push Sherlock very far, but maybe eventually we'd explore some of those avenues just the two of us.

"I suppose that's as good a reason as any," Sherlock said with a glint in his eyes that looked a tad mischievous.

I grinned back and gunned the engine.

CHAPTER THREE

Jemma

The wind rustled through the treetops as I studied the laptop's screen where I was sitting on the hood of the rental car, connecting the final pieces of a perfect scheme. The internet connection wasn't great here on the side of a lonely country road, but I got enough to both text with our prospective buyer and use the tracking software to confirm his general location.

I just needed to keep the guy communicating a bit longer. That was fine. I'd like to get a little more out of him to ensure this plan's success.

You've got the numbers, I wrote. *It's a great stash. Let's talk payment.*

My texting partner named a figure that brought a smile to my lips. Not that I needed the money, but clearly the cultist recognized the value of getting this large a collection of supplies all at once. *I need a full guarantee that this deal will stay completely anonymous,* he added.

Only the driver and the truck—one of us will arrive to hand off the payment. If we see anyone else around, everything's off.

Of course. I totally understand. That's a good amount of cash, but we've had other similar offers. Care to sweeten the pot? My boss is a collector as well as an investor. Art, historic relics, any sort of curiosities—if you've got anything like that you could add as a trade, I can make sure the goods go to you.

That request would be all too easy for the shrouded folk's people. One of the main ways they made money was creating and selling unusual artifacts to black magic aficionados and students of the occult. As far as I knew, most of those artifacts didn't contain any real magic—the shrouded folk rarely imbued a permanent object with their power the way they had the dagger that had severed my contract—but hobbyists couldn't get enough of them.

As expected, the guy wrote back just a few seconds later. *I have a friend who deals in supposedly supernatural items. Would something like that appeal?*

Oh, absolutely. He's fascinated by the paranormal. What kind of items are we talking about?

I could include a talisman for good fortune and a protective brooch.

My computer pinged, the app showing a fuzzy ring on the map, from which the texts were being sent. My initial forays had been correct, then. We'd be able to sic the local police on these people without any problem now.

Excellent. Consider the deal made, then. We'll have the shipment tomorrow night around 11pm. Can do the exchange at midnight. Why don't you pick the spot to ease your worries?

The cultist mentioned a half-constructed townhouse development about fifty miles out from where I estimated the commune to be. Close but not too close. As I tapped in my agreement, a muscular figure slipped from between the trees by the car, so stealthily I only heard the faintest rasp of his feet over the ground.

"We've got to get going," Bash said, yanking open the car door on the driver's side. With his khaki pants and broad-brimmed hat, meant to make him look like a mere hiker, you wouldn't have thought he could pull off much gravitas, but his expression was deadly serious. "I think I got a little too close. A sentry started heading my way as if he'd heard something. I'd rather he thinks it was his imagination."

"Shit." I slid off the hood of the car with a lurch of my heart and dropped into the passenger seat an instant later. Bash tossed his hat in the back and gunned the engine. He yanked the wheel to swing the car around. We roared off, back toward civilization.

"Anyone nearby is definitely going to hear *that*," I said with a teasing arch of my eyebrow.

Bash chuckled. "I got a good head start on that amateur. No point in waiting until someone's close enough that they *would* hear, that's all."

"So you had me terrified for nothing." I shook my head at him.

His chuckle turned into a full-out laugh. "As if you're ever really scared of anything, Majesty."

"You obviously don't know me as well as you should if you say that." I could remember with all too much vivid clarity the panicked thump of my heart as I'd scrambled onto a tall boulder on the Chilean mountainside, knowing I'd either free myself from the fiends that had owned me my whole life or die in the next few minutes.

"Maybe I shouldn't have said that, then. More accurately, you're the bravest person I know."

That kind of compliment coming from a man who'd

been through military combat as a sniper and all sorts of disreputable dealings since then was enough to send a flutter of warmth through me. "All right. That I'll accept."

Bash turned the car onto the main highway. "Where are we heading? The hotel here or all the way back to London?"

I shifted lower in the leather seat, getting comfortable. "We'll stay here. The deal's going through tomorrow night. No point in going to the city just to turn around and come back."

"Is everything set up, then?"

"Just about. I think Garrett still has a few strings to pull, but it sounded as if everything's going smoothly on his end too." I folded my arms behind my head and allowed myself a satisfied smile. "I had no idea how easy a scheme like this could be to pull off with the right talents at my disposal. Maybe I should have brought cops into the operation sooner."

Bash let out a snort. "I think we've had plenty of police presence as it is the last few months. We got lots done when it was just you running the show and me taking care of everything else."

His tone was casual, but a thread of tension ran through it. I glanced over at him, noting the tightening of his hands on the steering wheel. This merging of resources hadn't come easily to him. It *had* been just the two of us working in close partnership for a long time. I couldn't blame him for being hesitant—I'd certainly hesitated to put any trust in our trio at all. On the other hand…

"I'm not sure you should be criticizing the approach when you're the one who arranged it."

Bash's gaze jerked from the road to me. "What?" he said, but there was a hint of guilt in the flex of his jaw.

I waved my hand vaguely at him. "Don't give me that. Did you think I wouldn't figure out that you tipped the three of them off at least partly so they could find us in Chile? I've had plenty of time to think over every step we made and the precautions I took. They definitely didn't track us all that way in the space of a week because *I* let anything slip. Are you going to deny it now?"

His jaw worked again, and then he sighed. "Are you going to be angry? I saw how the situation was wearing on you. I wanted you to have as much backup as possible for your big plan. And after seeing how things went down during the eclipse, I still don't think I could have protected you by myself."

"Maybe not." The events after I'd concluded my ritual with the dagger were kind of a blur, but I knew the shrouded folk who'd turned up had come close to killing me. "You trusted the trio that much. Don't you trust them now?"

"It's not so much about trust," he muttered. "They just don't have the same perspective we do. We'll never be able to talk openly about half the things we're working on. It was only…" He sighed, and his voice gentled. "*I* was scared, all right. I was terrified of seeing anything happen to you. So I pulled out all the stops. That doesn't mean I can't want to push them back in now that they've done their job."

The words sent a softer wash of warmth through me. My hitman and I didn't discuss emotions very often. Until recently, we hadn't discussed them at all. Our loyalty to each other had been solid but unspoken.

Given recent events, the way Bash had stepped up for me, and the way my own perspective had shifted when it came to both the people in this world and what I might be capable of... I'd found I might have more capacity for caring in me than I'd ever have believed even half a year ago.

"I worry too, you know," I said. "About you and the others—about the danger I'm putting you in getting you involved in this mess with the shrouded folk. You've only scratched the surface of the sorts of horrors they enjoy."

"You focus on keeping yourself safe," Bash said firmly. "Let us decide for ourselves what we can handle—and I think we can handle a lot."

I gave him a crooked grin. "Do you want me to send them off or keep them a part of this, then? You can't have it both ways."

"Maybe not. I reserve the right to grumble about them anyway."

"Fair enough." His musky smell filled my lungs with my next breath, and I decided I could give him a larger show of devotion than simple words. I set my hand on his thigh and let my smile turn coy. "I can tell you that you're the only one *I'd* trust to stay steady while I do this."

"Do wha—fuck." His voice dropped to a whisper with the curse as my fingers brushed over his cock through his pants. With another stroke, he was already getting hard, swelling and stiffening at my touch.

The thrill made my smile stretch wider. Bash was the most unflappable person I'd ever met. I knew he could keep enough of his attention on the road even during my attentions to avoid a crash. But damn if it didn't turn me on a hundredfold to know how much of a thrill I could give *him*.

I gripped him harder, and he swallowed audibly, his gaze trained straight ahead. He shifted a couple inches lower in his seat to give me a better angle for access. I took advantage of the new position to pop open his fly. My hand delved beneath the fabric to uncover his rigid length, and Bash let out a low groan.

"There are still plenty of things we can do, just the two of us," I murmured, clicking open my seatbelt. Then I bent over and slicked my tongue around the head of his cock.

"God, Mori," Bash said in a ragged voice. Strength radiated all through his well-built body. I took him all the way into my mouth, reveling in the rough sound he made, in the slight buck of his hips toward me.

There'd been a time when I'd been afraid to give in to my attraction to Bash, even after I'd been sure he returned it. I'd only ever called on physical intimacy as one tool in my repertoire for getting what I wanted. I'd been afraid I might end up using him rather than being a real partner to him, falling into old habits. But in a moment like this, I knew there was no intention in me other than to show him just how happy I was to have him in my life.

The engine thrummed, and I moved my mouth in time, swirling my tongue over his silky skin and gripping the base of his cock. The salty, musky flavor of him flooded my mouth. I sucked him harder, and his elbow quivered where he'd let it rest lightly on my shoulder. With the pump of my hand and a swift flick across his tip, his breath hitched.

Heat pooled between my own legs. I pressed my thighs together as I took Bash down to the back of my throat. There'd be plenty of time to think about my own pleasure after I'd given him every bit I—

Bash's arm dropped abruptly, shielding my head as he yanked the wheel with his other hand. With a screech of tires, he pulled the car onto the shoulder. As I raised my head in confusion, he slammed on the parking brake and shoved his seat back. Then he tugged me all the way onto him, pulling my mouth to his.

Our lips collided in a mad crash. He tangled his fingers in my hair, tilting my head so he could kiss me even more deeply, while his other hand wrenched up my skirt and made short work of my panties. He caressed his thumb over my clit, sending a jolt of pleasure through me, and then dipped lower. At the slickness that spoke of my own desire, he growled against my mouth.

"If I'm going to come inside you, it's going to be here," he said, cupping my sex.

I gasped my giddy agreement. "Do you have—"

"I've decided to always be prepared." He dug a foil packet out of his pocket and ripped it open at lightning speed. I kissed him again, my tongue teasing over his, as he readied himself. The second I felt his hand draw back, I gripped him like I had when I'd been pleasuring him earlier and lowered myself onto his cock.

That first burn of bliss as he filled me was always a rush. Bash groaned again and kissed me with even more fervor. He'd almost been at the point of release already, and it didn't take more than a few thrusts to get me close too.

I fumbled for the seat control and tipped it all the way back so he was nearly lying down. As I braced my hands on either side, rocking up and down over him, he massaged my breasts through my blouse. Pleasure shot through my chest to meet the wave rising from my core.

The first time we'd had sex, he'd let me have my fun on top and then rolled me over to take charge. Today, he let me set the pace the whole way through. As the bliss rushed higher and my eyes started to roll back, his breath broke into panting, but he didn't make the slightest move toward unseating me.

That realization tipped me over the edge. As I careened into ecstasy, I tightened the muscles inside me to squeeze him harder. Bash grunted and pumped up to meet me, spilling himself alongside my peak.

I sagged over him, resting my forehead against his, and he gave me the most brilliant grin I'd ever seen cross his face. My heart sang and ached at the same time.

He was the most unflappable man I'd ever met, but he was willing to hand all control over to me. It *was* a little scary, no matter what he said. He'd given himself over to me completely in so many ways.

I had to make sure he never regretted it.

CHAPTER FOUR

Garrett

There were some things I loved about Scotland Yard. It was one place that was truly my own, for example. No matter how many cases Sherlock and John had a hand—or even the lion's share—in solving, I had my badge and they didn't. I'd put in the time and training to earn a spot here, and that meant something. For the most part, the people here believed in bringing crooks to justice by following the letter as well as the intention of the law, with a lot less of the moral blurring that the independent detectives dabbled in.

That said, sometimes I wished the place were a little less rigid and conformist—and that so many of my colleagues, stung by the fact that I'd been promoted ahead of them, weren't so eager to point out any area where I'd misstepped.

Thompson was still friendly enough, but I'd seen that jealous gleam in his eyes now and then, getting starker with each year that passed while he was still only detective constable. He ambled over to my desk as I finished up my phone call, his doughy face set with anticipation. My stomach twisted.

"Perfect," I said to the inspector on the other end. "It sounds like you've got everything in order there. I'm glad we could help."

Thompson propped himself against the side of my desk as I hung up. "Were you on the phone with Cumbria again?"

"Just passing on a few final details," I said briskly. "My informant heard a couple more things I thought they'd find useful in their sting operation."

"Seems like you've been spending more time fighting their crimes for them than working on troubles here in London." He straightened up and gave me a playful cuff to the shoulder. "Remember your holiday is over, Lestrade. We need you on the cases here. I wouldn't be surprised if that's what the chief wants to talk to you about."

"He asked to see me?" Damn. I'd hoped I could sail through this initial scheme without involving any of my higher-ups.

Thompson motioned toward the chief's office with a jab of his thumb. "He said you should head on in as soon as you were off the phone."

Well, the mission I'd gotten myself wrapped up in was only going to get more complicated as we continued rooting out Jemma's cult. I couldn't even say it was Jemma's mission now. From what I'd seen of her shrouded folk, the creatures stirred up far more violence and horror than any human criminal I'd ever encountered. I'd gone into this line of work to make a difference for good in the world. I couldn't have asked for a clearer opportunity.

And if I also found it hard to walk away from the

woman who both fascinated and unnerved me, no one else needed to know that part of the story.

Chief Higgins looked up from the report on his desk as I stepped into the office. He gestured for me to close the door. He'd been the chief as long as I'd worked at Scotland Yard, but he looked more the stereotypical brute enforcer than an administrative type, built like an ox, his ginger curls cropped close to his head. He was almost always frowning. You basically had to hang the moon—and the perpetrator of a decades-old unsolved case—before the man would crack a smile.

"Lestrade," he said. "I gather you've been coordinating rather a lot with the Cumbria Constabulary in the last few days."

"I have, sir," I said with a respectful bob of my head. The chief might be dour-faced most of the time, but in my experience, he was generally even-handed. "I came across information regarding a crime that I felt they should be aware of."

"You seem to have taken a particular interest in that crime. Is there some sort of personal stake I should be aware of?"

The memory of Jemma pressed up against me, her gasp in my ear, flickered through my mind with a flush of heat I managed to suppress. This was the perfect opening to start warming the chief up to the sort of cases I hoped to continue pursuing from my position here.

"Not personal," I said. "But I do feel a sort of responsibility. As the details came together, I realized this case appears to connect to that crime Holmes and I ended up investigating during our travels."

"Just like the both of you to go on vacation and end

up working harder than ever," Higgins muttered. "What was that again—a kidnapping?"

I hadn't gone into much detail about our exploits in Croatia with the department on my return, wanting to wait for the most strategic timing. This would appear to be it.

"We were looking into a missing persons case," I said, "but we ended up uncovering a far bigger problem. There was a cult operating in an area of wilderness near the coast —they'd been responsible for the murder of multiple children as well as more minor crimes like thefts."

The chief sat up straighter at my words. "A cult murdering children? That sounds like something out of a penny thriller."

"I know. I wish it hadn't been real." I still did. The thought of the evidence we'd uncovered about the commune's activities sent a chill through me even now.

"How does that relate to this crime in the Lake District?"

"We've seen a few similar patterns, sir. Certain types of thefts at a certain frequency, unusual disturbances in the same general area… We have reason to believe that the sect we stumbled on in Croatia was only one pocket of the cult, not the entire thing. Now Holmes and I suspect there may be at least one sect of the same group here in England."

Higgins' frown pulled deeper. "I can see why you'd have taken an interest, then. Not the sort of types we want in this country, that's for sure. Are there any signs we should keep an eye out for here in the city?"

"Not as far as I know yet," I said. "They seem to prefer to live in isolation. If something comes up, though, I'll let you know."

We could eventually let police departments all across the world know, couldn't we? Why should the five of us be the only ones tracking down signs of the cult? The clues were simple enough to follow once you were familiar with the pattern.

Once we took down this sect here on home ground—once we'd proven they had a presence everywhere from here to Croatia—those other departments would have to take notice. We could send out briefs all over the place, and they'd do most of our work for us.

Of course, we couldn't trust that they'd all take the same sort of care that Jemma wanted. Simply sending the cultists on the run wouldn't do the job, from what she'd said—they needed to be caught and confined. But perhaps we could come up with strategies for ensuring the right approach was taken even if we weren't directly involved. Surely she didn't expect to personally tackle every single commune of the dozens or even hundreds she'd indicated might exist?

"Well," the chief said. "I'm glad you're keeping an ear to the ground on this subject. It does your policing instincts credit."

I couldn't stop a smile from springing to my lips at the praise, which Higgins doled out only sparingly. I might have proven myself quite a bit by earning the position of detective inspector at a younger age than anyone else currently working here had, but this was an entirely different level of policing. My scope had shifted from merely the city to a threat that encompassed the world— and I was bringing Scotland Yard on board with it.

At least, I'd made a *small step* toward bringing the Yard on board. Higgins followed up his praise with a firm stare. "It sounds as though you've done all you can for Cumbria now. I want your focus back on your regular duties from here on. We have no shortage of our own cases that need tending to."

"Yes," I said, my smile faltering. "Absolutely. I was just looking through the Shawfend file a few minutes ago, actually."

"See if you can't crack that one, then. And feel free to rope Holmes in if you take a mind to. Heaven knows if you can catch his interest with a crime, he'll find his way to the answer faster than any of us could."

My tone flattened slightly. "Yes. I'm not sure it's quite unusual enough to pique his interest. I can sort it out without the extra help."

"I know you can," the chief said, easing the sting of his earlier remark. "Well, what are you waiting for? Get on with it."

He sent me from his office with a shooing motion. I managed not to grimace as I headed out. Several pairs of eyes watched me return to my desk. A prickle ran down my back.

There was taking policing to a higher level and tackling widespread brutality, and then there was looking like an obsessed lunatic. I was going to have to be careful I didn't stray into the latter territory.

There was so much I couldn't tell anyone here: not my colleagues, not the chief. Keeping the supernatural elements they'd never believe—that I barely believed even having experienced them directly—a secret was only going to get harder as the five of us dug deeper into this hornets' nest. I'd often prided myself on being straightforward, a man you could assume would cut to the chase. My association with Jemma had turned me into a conspirator.

All the same, the current London cases were hardly

gripping enough to hold *my* attention all that well when I had demonic beings and murderous cults on the brain. I took some notes and talked to the constable who'd interviewed a couple of the witnesses, and then set off to consider the scene of the robbery myself. By the time my shift was over, I was itching to be off in the Lake District with the others.

They were meant to be closing in on the commune there tonight, and I couldn't have any direct part in it. I'd already stretched the department's patience with my extended vacation.

My phone rang just as I came into my flat. I glanced at the number with a jolt of excitement that quickly faded.

"Hello, Mum," I said as I answered it.

My mother's high voice carried through the line. "Garrett! I hope I'm not interrupting anything. I know how busy you get."

"I'm done work for the day," I told her, sinking down onto my sofa—which was starting to get rather threadbare in spots, I noticed. I really ought to find the time to go shopping for a new one. "How are you?"

She rambled on for a few minutes about her garden, her book club, and the nurse at her medical practice, and I hummed encouragingly at appropriate moments. I'd never totally felt like a part of the Lestrade family, if I was being honest. Even to look at the lot of us, you'd see me as cut from a different cloth. My parents and older brothers were all blond and brighter eyed, and they'd gravitated toward the sorts of professions that elegant people at the dinner parties they often held would exclaim admiringly over.

I'd turned out darker and wiry and often sullen. I hadn't excelled in school. No one in the house had really known what to do with me. And I'd felt it, so deeply something sharp still stirred inside me if I let myself linger on that thought too long.

"Anyway," Mum said finally, "we were thinking we'd have all of you over the weekend after next for dinner. Can you make it on the Saturday?"

It took me a second to catch up. "All of us?"

"You and your brothers," she said in a familiar faintly exasperated tone.

"Oh. Yes—yes, I should be able to manage that."

Even as I said the words, my heart was sinking. It was ridiculous. Any wrongs I'd done were well over a decade ago. None of my brothers had any idea I'd ever caused them any harm with my childhood pranks anyway.

I knew, though. I knew they'd been not so much pranks but malicious acts propelled by jealousy. I'd been as bad as the colleagues who watched my moves in the office so carefully.

That was why I worked so bloody hard, wasn't it? Surely I'd made enough amends to counterbalance the pain I'd brought into the world by now.

And if I hadn't, destroying a realm's worth of demons should do the trick all right.

CHAPTER FIVE

Jemma

The gold cuff formed a constant pressure around my thigh as Bash and I crept through the dark forest. The metal artifact wasn't diminishing my body the way it had when I'd been wearing it for weeks before, but the feel of it summoned the memory of the shocks of pain and the fading of my skin.

Thank goodness for Sherlock's coolheadedness in grabbing the pieces, because it would keep me undetected by our supernatural foes during our schemes, but I couldn't wait to take it off. I didn't expect any of the folk to be prowling around at night, when their powers in this world were at their weakest, but I wasn't taking any chances.

Only slivers of moonlight and my memory of my earlier scouting missions guided our way. I stopped at the sight of a small notch in the bark of a tree. It easily passed for the scrape of some small animal's claws, but I'd marked it there yesterday with a pocket knife.

"Start here," I whispered to Bash, and pointed to the notch. "You'll find a mark about every ten feet. We want this whole end of the perimeter covered."

He nodded, shifting the large knapsack he'd been carrying off his back. It was full of coils of wire, so thin and dark it wouldn't show up against the night's thick shadows, twisted and barbed to not just trip but snare anyone who ran into it.

The cultists would flee when the police arrived. I aimed to be sure they didn't make their escape successfully.

I touched Bash's arm briefly as I moved to leave, and he gave me the small knowing smile I'd only ever seen aimed at me. The smile that said he had no doubt I'd accomplish exactly what I was setting out to do, and he was looking forward to celebrating my victory on the other side.

He started fixing the end of the wire around the base of the tree trunk. I slunk on, closer to the spot where the commune's farthest sentries would be lurking. As I went, I slid on the night vision goggles Bash had obtained for me.

This cult settlement appeared to be a fairly subdued one, no major troubles recently, so they probably wouldn't have had a substantial guard most of the time. Tonight, though, with one of their own off arranging a criminal deal, I'd expect their security to be doubled.

I didn't want the inhabitants getting much in the way of advance warning of the raid. My job was to dispatch the sentries quickly and quietly. As a bonus, I could plant a few clues on their body to help speed justice along once the police found them.

I set my feet down with care, avoiding twigs and loose rocks, keeping close to the trees. My stark red hair might have drawn attention even in the dim moonlight, but I'd tucked it under the hood of my light jacket. My skin was starting to sweat with the late summer heat, still present in the middle of the night, but I kept all my attention focused on the forest ahead of me.

There. The goggles picked up the form of a middle-aged man with a holster at his hip as he shifted his weight at the edge of a little clearing up ahead. I paused for a moment, taking in his stance, the position of his gun, and the movement of his attention. Then I slipped closer.

No one else moved in the woods as I circled around him. I eased across the uneven ground until I was just a short leap away. He raised his gun hand to scratch at his scalp, and I sprang.

I'd told the trio that I wasn't going to try to kill *all* of the cultists, but I hadn't made any promises about a handful here and there. This guy would only cease to be a threat if I put him totally out of commission.

As I caught him, I grasped his jaw and the side of his head. Before he could let out more than a grunt of surprise, I wrenched my arms. His neck snapped, and his body slumped. I lowered him to the ground.

One down, I'd guess at least four more to go.

I stuffed my bit of "evidence" in his shirt pocket and stalked on. The guards closest to the dirt road that led into the commune were my main concern. I found another posted by a garage building where the road petered out, and dispatched her as swiftly as the first guy.

I didn't have much space in me for conscience, given the life I'd led and the things I'd had to do to make sure I stayed alive. The people whose lives *I* was taking tonight had sacrificed children to monsters and encouraged everyone around them to carve themselves up in worship. Still, a twinge that felt almost like guilt passed through my gut as I came up on the third guard, a young man with fawn-brown hair like Garrett's.

What would my trio have thought if they'd witnessed the crimes I was committing tonight? They'd seen the results of my efforts when they'd stormed the commune in Croatia, but only after a shoot-out between the police and the cultists. There wouldn't have been any telling which bodies were my fault.

If they'd watched me walk up to this guy, slam my knuckles into the back of his head, and crack his neck as coolly as if he were a chicken for a roast, would they have looked at me with anything other than horror?

Possibly not. That was why Bash balked at keeping them around, wasn't it? He trusted them to help but not to understand, and he was right. If they'd been through what I had—if they'd understood how the shrouded folk had taken over these people and how many more lives would be lost if I couldn't see through my mission—

It didn't do me any good thinking about it.

The thought lingered with me, though—enough that I paused when I spotted the next sentry. This one was a young woman, barely more than a girl really. Only a few years older than I'd been when I'd fled my family's commune back in Utah. Old enough to have survived past the sacrificial age and to have become fully complicit, of course. Still, something clenched in my chest as I studied her. She rubbed her thin lips, scanning the forest around her with a twitchy gaze.

It wasn't as if I *enjoyed* killing. Take the shrouded folk out of the picture, and I'd have been perfectly happy never harming another human being—other than separating the undeserving from some of their money every now and then as need be—for the rest of eternity.

I hadn't spent much time considering what my life might look like after I removed the shrouded folk from this world. It was hard to imagine that time or that I'd make it through the entire mission alive. But survival seemed a little more likely now. I might be able to look forward to much less fraught times in the distant future.

I shouldn't have let myself dwell on those ideas. They threw off my concentration. This time, even though the girl was clearly the least experienced of the guards I'd tackled, I held back just a little as I grabbed her from behind. The tiny hesitation left just enough of an opening for her to cry out and jab her elbow into my stomach.

Pain burst through my abdomen. My body reacted on pure instinct after that. I slapped my hand over her mouth to prevent any louder shouts for help or of warning and yanked her head to the side so fast my shoulders burned with the effort.

Her spine snapped. Her body sagged like all the others. I laid her down with a trickle of queasiness both at the task I'd had to carry out and my own momentary faltering.

What good was it being human, caring about other humans, if that would mean the shrouded folk kept strewing their misery and violence? No, I was exactly the way I needed to be right now, and if my trio ended up having a problem with that, the door was always open for them to leave.

I turned on my heel, studying the woods around me, my ears perked for any sound—any indication that the girl's brief cry had drawn attention. Nothing stirred. The next sentry, if there even was another, must have been far enough away. I exhaled in relief and was just moving on in my sweep of the forest when engines rumbled behind me.

I spun with a lurch of my heart, but my pulse settled in an instant. The flash of headlights carried from the road I'd passed, showing the colors of a line of police cars arriving. The cavalry was here.

That was my cue to fade away. The local police didn't know anything about my involvement in this sting operation, and it was better for everyone if we kept it that way.

I turned to head for the spot where I was supposed to meet Bash at the car, and a whiff of a scent reached my nose that set the hairs on the back of my neck on end. Dry and sour like something dead so long it'd mummified— that was the smell that clung to the shrouded folk. None of those fiends could sense my presence with the gold cuff shielding me, but I could pick up on theirs just fine.

The odor could have simply lingered from when the folk had moved through and around the commune during the previous day, but I hadn't noticed it earlier. That suggested this waft was fresh. Despite the lack of sunlight, at least one shrouded one's attention had been drawn back to our world by the growing commotion descending on their worshippers.

What the hell did it mean to do?

The police cars had parked around the garage. Officers poured out of them and hustled with guns drawn along the narrower footpath that led to the commune. I made out Sherlock's tall, thin frame and John's broader form amid the uniforms.

Another whisper of the shrouded-folk scent drifted past me. I grimaced and treaded carefully after the flood of cops.

The fiends *shouldn't* interfere with this operation. There were too many witnesses; the risk of discovery too high. But they'd been desperate enough in Chile to attack me in front of the crowd that had gathered to watch the eclipse. I wasn't sure I trusted them to follow their own laws at this point. And if one of them was up to something, none of the officers who were storming the compound had any idea how to deal with them.

Shouts were ringing out now. A couple of cops led figures in handcuffs back to the cars. The crack of a gunshot split the air, and I restrained a flinch. Oh, yes, the police were convinced this commune was a den of criminals now.

I stopped several feet back from the sparser patch of forest where the commune had set up their cabins. Flashlights cast their beams all through the area, catching on the walls and the nauseated faces of the cops making gruesome discoveries. As they hustled more people off, one of them emerged from a building and promptly vomited beside the doorway. I was going to guess that was the bloodletting room.

I edged around the settlement until I spotted my consulting detective and his sidekick again. Sherlock was motioning to something on the ground while a few of the cops looked on, John nodding enthusiastically as if his show of agreement would make whatever the other man was saying easier to swallow. One of the cops knelt down —and a flicker of light that hadn't come from any flashlight glanced off the leaves over Sherlock's head.

A cry of warning caught in my throat. If I rushed in there without any good reason to be in the area, I'd force my two allies to make up a big story about what I was doing at the commune that would complicate everything. I tensed, watching to see if the shrouded one would actually make a move.

The light wavered and then vanished. I'd just started to relax when Sherlock's arm twitched. He slapped his forearm as if to catch a mosquito, and I sprang a few steps forward before I realized there was nothing more to the apparent "attack." If he'd been reacting to the shrouded one, it'd barely touched him.

I stayed there, braced to leap in if the fiends made another move, as Sherlock returned to his work. He didn't pay his arm any more mind. But even from where I stood, I could see a purplish mark coming into focus on the skin just below his wrist. My hands clenched at my sides.

The shrouded one *had* touched him. What were the fiends playing at now?

CHAPTER SIX

Jemma

Garrett made a disgruntled sound and sprawled deeper into the corner of Sherlock and John's sofa. "I wish I could have made it up there for the takedown."

"No, you don't," John said from the other end of the sofa, with an uncharacteristically grim expression. "The things those people do, the evidence we uncovered just in the initial sweep…" His lips twisted at a sickly angle. "And all this time these creatures have been pushing people to savage each other right under our noses."

Sherlock had stayed on his feet for this meeting, pacing now with a soft rasp of his shoes over the rug. In the early afternoon light steaming through the living room's two narrow windows, his light blue eyes glittered even more coolly than usual. "Not any longer. We're bringing them to justice just as we've gone so many other criminals, even if the others were human. It makes no difference."

I shifted in the stiffly padded armchair I'd taken—I

could tell just from the rigid feel of it that it was probably Sherlock's usual perch. "That's not entirely true. Let me see your right arm?"

He hesitated for a second before moving toward me when I beckoned him over. That was enough to tell me that he already knew what I was after. Even though it was another warm summer day and only a whirring fan added any relief to the heat in the apartment, he'd chosen a long-sleeved button-up to wear today. With a pointed look, I motioned for him to roll up the sleeve.

"I bumped my arm against something while we were searching the commune," he said briskly. "I suppose you saw that from the outskirts before you left."

"You didn't bump it against something," I informed him. "Something bumped against you. More specifically, a shrouded one."

I took his wrist gingerly, studying the mark that had formed like a bruise on his forearm. If I hadn't seen it happen, I might have taken it for an actual bruise. Because I knew to look for the signs, I noticed the faint, erratic dappling along the edges.

And when I breathed in, the dry rotten scent I'd first picked up in the forest still tainted the air.

"One of them marked you," I said. "I don't know why, but it'll have left a little of its energy in you so it can track you down again."

Bash leaned farther over the back of my chair, where he'd propped his sculpted arms. "Why would they want to do that? Why him?"

"Maybe word has spread enough that it recognized you had something to do with the incident in Chile," I said to Sherlock. "Or in Croatia, for that matter. They'd have wanted an easy way to trace you back to me, or at least to keep an eye on you even if you didn't. Hold on."

I got up and moved to the dining table. One of the napkins from our takeout lunch would do. I ripped it into even pieces and started spreading them across the wooden surface of the sideboard in a Fibonacci pattern.

John got up from the sofa to watch my progress. "You did that in my hotel room during the conference."

I nodded. "The shrouded folk thrive on pain and unpredictability. The certainty of mathematical patterns throws them off. This won't stop one that's particularly determined, but it'll act as a general deterrent—and it may even interfere somewhat with their ability to tune into the energy in that mark. Leave this here."

"I suppose it makes for an interesting decoration," Sherlock said with a lift of his eyebrows.

He wasn't taking this problem seriously enough. I went back to the chair and grabbed my purse. "I also think that for the time being, you should wear this. You should be fine for a week or two without any ill effects, and maybe that'll be long enough for them to give up on you."

I offered him the pieces of the gold cuff. Sherlock blinked at them and raised his gaze to my face.

"You need these," he said. "You're their primary target."

"Yeah," Garrett said. "We already know they'll try to hurt *you*, even with the contract broken."

"They came after all of you when you were getting me out of the way after the ritual, didn't they?" I shook the pieces at Sherlock. "You're the one they're the most interested in right now. If they follow you to me, then I'm screwed anyway."

The detective's lips pursed, but he accepted the cuff. After examining the pieces, he rolled up his pantleg and fiddled with them until he'd secured them around his lower thigh. Then he raised his eyebrows at me. "Satisfied?"

"Reasonably. Make sure it stays there."

Garret shot Sherlock a quick glower as if he blamed the other man for giving in to my demand. "What are the next steps, then?" he asked me.

"Last night's raid will have stirred things up all through the cult, especially any other local sects," I said. "For a few days, we can monitor the various types of activity around the other locations you thought looked like possibilities. I suspect we'll see some indications confirming one or more of those, and then we can move ahead from there."

We discussed who would collect which data for several more minutes. By the time I got up to leave, the rancid scent had faded from the air. The cuff and my sequence must have been enough to put off any shrouded folk hanging around here, if one had stuck around after following Sherlock to the apartment at all.

Garrett looked as though he intended to stick around, but he caught my arm before I headed out after Bash. His dark brown eyes searched mine. "Are you sure *you* have enough protections, firecracker? If I can get you anything…"

I didn't know if there *was* anything a police officer had access to that would fend off the shrouded folk, and from his pained expression he didn't either. But the offer and the affectionately admiring nickname softened the tension inside me anyway.

"I've been keeping myself safe for ten years," I

reminded him. "I've got all the methods down pat. But thank you."

I tugged him a little closer to kiss him as consolation for my refusal. Garrett stiffened for a second, most likely in awareness of his friends still in the room, but it wasn't as if my widespread affections were any secret among this bunch.

He'd been the first of the trio I'd drawn in, the first who'd really cared about me, and as silly as the consideration sometimes seemed, part of me was determined never to make him feel he came in second place.

He relaxed into the kiss, touching the side of my face as he kissed me back hard. The heat of his mouth sang through me. It was an awful shame I had illicit activities to plan right now that my police officer wouldn't want to be privy to.

"To be continued," I told him in a teasing voice as I drew back, and headed out with a smile on my lips.

Bash had waited for me in the hall outside. "Where are you off to now, Majesty?" he asked in a dry tone as we headed for the stairs, but his eyes studied me with concern. Apparently all my men were in protective mode at the moment.

"Back to my place and the computer for at least the next little bit," I said. "I'll let you know if I think we need to take another field trip."

A hint of acrid rot touched my nose, and I tried not to let him see me tense. Oh, one of the fiends had stuck around, clearly. And now it was following me.

"Why don't I join you?" Bash tipped his head toward the street. "Two minds accomplish more than one?"

They might, but whatever the shrouded folk might

intend for me, he didn't have anywhere near the practice at defending himself that I did. Neither did Sherlock, which was why I'd insisted he take the cuff. If the fiends were going to break their rules and make themselves known, dealing with them was my responsibility. My allies had already put themselves in plenty of danger as it was.

I tapped Bash's solid chest. "I suspect in this particular case it'd be more a matter of two bodies creating too many distractions. Besides, I need you to follow up with our forger about that payment."

Bash's jaw tightened. I grasped his arm and bobbed up to give him a quick kiss, heading off any further argument he might have made. "I'll see you soon," I said. "You know how to reach me if anything urgent comes up."

I hailed a taxi in the vague hope that a car might throw the fiend off, but I didn't really expect that to work. The shrouded folk scent met me as soon as I stepped out onto the sidewalk outside the posh modern apartment building where I'd gotten a short-term, furnished rental unit. I pretended not to notice and marched on inside.

I quite liked the place I'd gotten with its clean simple lines and muted color palette of ivory and soft grays, but it was hard to get comfortable knowing I had an unwelcome visitor. I'd already laid out a few Fibonacci sequences in the decorative stones that had come in a glass bowl on the hall table. They obviously hadn't been enough to shake my follower. I tweaked them slightly in at attempt to improve their accuracy and wandered into the bedroom to grab my laptop.

When I came back into the open-concept main room, a hazy figure shrouded in strips of pale streamers was waiting for me, hovering over the coffee table. I stopped dead in my tracks, my heart lurching even though I'd been expecting something like this.

It was impossible to tell the shrouded folk apart by physical characteristics. They didn't have much of a bodily presence in our world at all. With a person, I'd have considered the facial features, but all the shrouded folk had where their faces should be was a gaping black void amid the folds of tattered fabric—or perhaps it was swaths of dead skin. What a pleasant thought.

Still, in the first instant as I took in the visitor, I knew it wasn't the one I'd called Bog—the one I'd made a deal with to get me out of my commune in the first place. The quiver of energy in the air and the exact taint of the dryly putrid scent wasn't quite the same. When you'd lived among the fiends for fourteen years of your life, you learned other ways of identifying them.

"Not much for manners, are you?" I said to this one in the most flippant tone I could summon. "Guests are generally supposed to wait for an invitation. A knock would have been a good start too."

The shrouded one spoke with a voice as dry as its scent and utterly emotionless. "We do not bother with doors."

"Clearly." I flopped down on the linen sofa. "What do you want, then? I don't owe any of you anything now. All contracts have been voided."

"Indeed." Its form shifted as if it were gathering itself. "But you voided them by way of a trick. And even if we might have ignored that and left you alone, *you* have not left *us* alone."

"I don't recall doing anything to any shrouded folk."

"Do not play games. You are interfering with our worshippers and drawing other humans into this purpose. To what end?"

I fixed my gaze on the area where its eyes should have been. "What do you *think*?"

"You will not stop then."

Its tone was too flat for the sentence to be a question, but I answered it anyway. "I'll do whatever the hell I want, and none of you get to have any say in it. Not so fun being on the receiving end of that treatment, is it?"

The shrouded one quivered. "I think you are mistaken in how much control you have over this situation."

"I know your laws. I know the ones who came at me and my colleagues with physical force two weeks ago will have been sanctioned. I'm not the one who revealed that you exist to them—you all did that by yourselves."

"Yes, but there are forces other than the physical, as you should well know. I don't intend to leave you alone, not at all, not for as long as you still exist."

I tensed instinctively as the words drifted out into the air. The room around me was already mutating. A red slick spread across the peachy hardwood floor like a pool of blood, and then another formed on the other side of the coffee table, then another by kitchen island.

A metallic scent filled the air. But Bog had tried a bloody hallucination on me before, and I'd survived that. I fixed my gaze on the shrouded one in front of me.

"Is that the best you've got?"

It didn't speak, didn't move other than the erratic wavering of its covering as if the fabric were floating in an uncertain current, but I could have sworn I tasted a smile in that instant.

The puddles rippled. A bulge formed in the tops of them. It rose larger, the blood streaking down the emerging form until my spine stiffened in recognition.

My sister's face. Olivia's head—no, her whole body—

was emerging from each of the crimson pools. Just as young as she'd been the last time I'd seen her, when she'd been ten and I'd been fourteen and I'd given her one last desperate kiss to the cheek before I'd fled, promising her I'd come back for her.

I'd been too late. The guilt of that fact never left me, and right now it knotted tight all through my chest.

There were five of her—no, six, seven, eight—rising up like cherubic demons summoned from the underworld. Her blood-streaked eyelids opened. Her bright blue eyes fixed on me from all sides. Her lips pulled back in a horrifying grimace.

"You did this to me," she wailed, all of her at once. "You killed me. It was you."

One of the heads popped off with a nauseating squelch. Another spun around as her neck purpled with bruises. One dug her hand right into her blood-splattered dress and gouged her heart out of her chest. Bile shot up my throat.

I closed my eyes and covered my face, focusing on the pattern of my breathing, but the rasp in and out had turned shaky.

"You. Murderer. I hate you!" she ranted, her thin voice carrying on and on. Something wet and squishy smacked into my hair—for fuck's sake, had one of the illusions thrown her own heart at my head?

Under my breath, I started reciting the decimals of pi. I'd made it to the seventh when one of my sister's bodies flung itself right into me.

CHAPTER SEVEN

Sherlock

I'd followed a rather incredible number of individuals in my time, both outright criminals and ordinary people who simply had something to hide. Technically, Jemma was the former, as much as I disliked that fact. She was certainly the most formidable target I'd ever tailed.

I'd made a couple of hasty changes to my appearance before I'd headed out after her: a swipe of gel through my hair to both darken it and slick it back, a pair of prescriptionless glasses from one of the drawers in the side table. As I ambled out onto the street, I let my posture slouch to disguise my height and thinness. My stride took on the rolling gait of a much portlier man.

Very few people who'd ever met me would have recognized me in passing, and I doubted even Jemma would have identified me on first glance. There was a much higher chance that she'd realize *someone* was following her, regardless of whom, and so when I spotted her flaming red hair just a few dozen feet farther up the street where she was speaking with Moran, I turned and began sauntering in the opposite direction.

A tiny mirror embedded in one side of the glasses allowed me to keep an eye on her even from behind. Her conversation with her associate ended quickly. As she hailed a cab, I beckoned for one of my own.

"Follow that car there," I instructed the driver as soon as I'd slid into the back. "Police business."

I'd learned over the years that those last two words could prevent all sorts of hesitation, even if I wasn't officially employed by the police. Few people bothered to check. This fellow pulled away from the curb without a single question and kept on Jemma's trail as her cab wove through London's chaotic streets.

The gold artifact she'd insisted I put on pressed against my thigh. The thin metal wasn't exactly *un*comfortable, but I didn't feel entirely comfortable wearing it. The symbols etched in it and the gems embedded in the thin metal surface had some esoteric power that I barely understood—that a few weeks ago I wouldn't have believed was anything more than superstition.

I hadn't liked the impression I'd gotten from Jemma as she'd made to leave. She'd had an air of apprehension I doubted anyone else in the room had picked up on, she was so skilled at moderating her emotions and distracting those around her by stirring up other feelings. Nevertheless, the subtle signs had been noticeable enough to me now that I'd had ample time to observe her over recent months.

Something had been worrying her. She wouldn't have told me what if I'd asked. So I would find out the way I found out many things, through further observation and deduction.

I might have volunteered my support to her cause, and I might appreciate her dedication to ending the horrors we'd witnessed from this cult twice now, but that didn't mean I was going to trust her completely. I highly doubted her faith in the three of us on the right side of the law was anywhere close to unwavering.

Jemma didn't appear to be heading anywhere unusual at the moment. Her cab led us from Westminster into East London and stopped outside a posh white apartment building that rose several stories higher than its nearest neighbor. I'd already determined she'd rented a flat in the place. She'd only been returning to it.

I might have headed home myself then if I hadn't caught a glimpse of her face on her way out of the cab while my own idled farther down the street. Now that she believed she had no witnesses, her mouth was set in a tense line, and her gaze darted around her warily—not along the sidewalk or across the road but higher along the buildings.

She was watching for some threat she expected to come from above. I waited until she'd gone into the building, and then I handed the driver his payment and went after her.

I didn't know precisely which flat she was renting, but the elevator indicator helpfully told me which floor she'd gotten off on, and a quick sweep of that hallway gave me enough clues to deduce which door she'd gone through. I hesitated there, momentarily unsure of myself.

Jemma understood how I worked. If I knocked and explained myself, she'd almost certainly laugh and perhaps admit to the problem if I insisted. Although perhaps I should take a turn around the building first to see if I could unearth any signs of a potential threat for myself.

Before I'd quite decided, Jemma's voice carried through the door. The building was well-constructed enough to hold sound within each flat, but even though I couldn't make out the words, the sound had the tenor of a rising yell. I might have even detected an edge of panic to it.

My instincts kicked in. Without a second thought, I yanked out my wallet, grabbed a keycard one of my less reputable sources had provided me with some years ago, shoved it into the slot, and jammed on the handle at the same time.

The building might have been solid, but it was hardly military-level secure. Hitting the handle with the right angle and pressure in combination with the signal on the card disengaged the lock in an instant. I shoved the door open and hurtled inside.

Jemma was standing at the edge of her living room, her eyes closed, her hands thrust out at either side, her face sickly pale. Her yell was already fading, but her voice kept on chanting a stream of numbers I recognized as digits of pi. She motioned with her hands, and her shoulders came down a tad. She recited more digits even faster.

The sight of her so frantic set my own mind off-kilter. Jemma was the most self-possessed person I'd ever encountered. For something to have shaken her this badly—

It had to be something to do with those creatures, her shrouded folk.

My thoughts were still whirling, but there was one certain way I knew to combat the monsters. After all, she'd given it to me just an hour ago. I yanked up my trouser leg to snap open the gold cuff and rushed the rest of the way to her.

Jemma's eyes popped open as I knelt in front of her. I closed the cuff around her thigh over the fabric of her slacks, where it fit snugly. If I'd needed proof of the artifact's efficacy, it came with the rush of relief in her exhalation. She peered at me as I straightened up, the color already starting to come back into her cheeks, her eyebrows arching.

"Where did you come from all of a sudden, Sherlock?"

"I got the impression you might need some assistance." I studied the room around us, my stance tensing. Jemma might be protected now, but I no longer was. The bruise on my arm was evidence enough that the creatures were willing to affect me at least in small ways. "What happened?"

"One of the fiends showed up and tried to make me regret taking them on. It didn't work. I *was* getting a handle on the situation by myself, just so you know."

"By reciting numbers."

She ran her fingers through her hair, which had fallen astray during her distress. "Yes. I told you the shrouded folk don't like mathematical certainties." She dragged in a deep breath. "It made the hallucination the thing created ease off, and I think the fiend is gone now."

She had ways of detecting it beyond anything she could teach us or that I could fully understand. That knowledge made me shift restlessly on my feet, my own lungs tightening. These creatures exerted their horrible influence on our world in so many ways, could bring this magnificent woman to a state of panic in a matter of minutes, and even after tangling with them and their worshippers multiple times, they were still the biggest mystery I'd ever encountered, a vast blank in my understanding.

They left me little to observe, next to nothing to deduce from, and the deductions I could make jarred against everything logic and common sense offered.

"Are you safe to stay here?" I asked, with a prickle of frustration that I had no idea what the answer to that question might be.

"They can't affect me while the cuff is around my body," Jemma said. "Although of course that's why I gave it to *you*. I can fend for myself."

She bent down to remove it, clearly with the intention of giving it back to me. I caught her arm before she could.

"No," I said firmly when she glanced up at me. This much, at least, I was utterly certain of. "The things marked me yesterday, and they haven't harmed me in any way since then. The moment you no longer had that artifact in your possession, they came at you. There's nothing you can say that will convince me that I need it more than you do."

She sighed. "Fine. Let me at least put it out of sight. It's more effective skin to skin anyway."

I let go of her so she could unclasp the cuff and slip it under her slacks. The sight of her leg bare halfway up her thigh set off a flicker of heat that shot from my chest to my groin. The sensation of lust wasn't one I was especially familiar with either, but at least it wasn't a mystery. On the contrary, it was a human weakness so commonplace I'd once prided myself in being above it.

Jemma had shown me the productive side of physical satisfaction. And I couldn't say there wasn't a certain sense of accomplishment in bringing a woman this brilliant and assured to the heights of pleasure.

Her eyebrow rose again as she let her pant leg slip back down, as if she suspected my reaction. Perhaps I'd given off some hint of it that she could read as easily as I read so much else. She looked around the room as if confirming there was no sign of whatever the creature had been tormenting her with, and another pinch of restlessness nipped at me.

This was the greatest case of my career by far. My opponent couldn't remain this opaque to me. Otherwise I'd be little more use in bringing the things to justice than a constable straight out of school.

"Will the same trick with the numbers work for anyone, should the creatures attempt a similar assault on the rest of us?" I asked.

"Yes, for anyone who has plenty of pi memorized." She grinned at me. "I suppose you've got it to the thousandth digit or so."

"Somewhere around there."

"I don't think we'll need to put that possibility to the test, though. They aren't afraid to hit me with the worst they can conjure up because I'm a known quantity—I used to belong to them. With the rest of you, they'll be more careful to follow their rules. If they come after you, it may be in ways so subtle you don't realize there's any supernatural influence at all."

She folded her arms over her chest. "I think I'd better come back to your apartment with you, if you're going to insist on leaving the cuff with me."

"I'd imagine John and I can take care of ourselves, especially if the effect would be so small."

"You of all people should know that subtle doesn't have to mean small. The shrouded folk only followed you there recently. I don't think I should leave you and John alone on your first night afterward, not until I see if they're planning anything more than just following."

I opened my mouth to protest again and paused. Why dismiss her help? It would be easier to learn the ways of these things with her there to guide us if one of them acted on us. I might have my pride, but only a stupid man would wave off the chance to learn vital information.

"All right," I said. "I suppose there's the couch, if you can accept sleeping there."

"I think I'll manage just fine," she said, with a glint in her eye that suggested she expected she'd make it into one or the other of our beds if only for a portion of the night. "Let me get a few things, and then we can start our monster watch."

Jemma

"Oooh, right *there*," I said, letting myself sink deeper into the sofa cushion.

John chuckled at the other end of the sofa, where he was massaging my foot with skilled strokes of his thumb. Each press sent a pleasant burn and a trickle of relaxation through the muscles all the way up my leg. Between that and the Indian takeout filling my belly, I couldn't imagine a much more enjoyable way to spend an evening. Perhaps I should look into bringing on the doctor as a full-time foot masseuse.

"Ready for the other one yet?" he asked with a lift of one eyebrow. I hadn't asked for the massage, but I had sprawled out on the sofa with my feet on his lap when we'd retired to the living room after dinner, so I supposed that'd seemed like enough of a prompt.

"No, I'll take a little more on the arch before you move on," I said with a grin.

Sherlock shook his head where he was sitting in the

armchair next to the sofa, pipe in hand and tablet propped on one knee, but the corners of his lips had quirked upward as well. "You'd better not let word get out how easily won over you are by a little foot rub. What will become of the brilliant Jemma Moriarty then?"

"She'll have incredibly well-tended-to feet," I shot back, and let out another encouraging hum as John dug his thumb in a little deeper just above my heel. The rich smell of Sherlock's pipe smoke mingled with the honey sweetness lingering in my mouth from the extensive dessert I'd ensured the takeout meal included, making another sort of heaven all on its own. Who needed a criminal empire when you could have this?

The thought had passed through my mind in jest, but a twinge followed it. My life *could* have looked something like this if I'd been born into a normal family, not one devoted to the shrouded folk and offering up their children as further sacrifice. If I'd had a chance to learn how to really connect with people instead of seeing them all as competition… If I hadn't been left with my sister's murder hanging over my head…

But then the world wouldn't have any Jemma Moriarty to carry out her avenging mission. The shrouded folk would still have existed, still have killed other children. On the balance, everyone else was better off for my fraught early years.

I wouldn't have minded a taste of that imaginary alternate life, though. This might be one right here. No unsettling scent had returned to the apartment to indicate a shrouded one had returned to survey it. There wasn't anything wrong in indulging in the illusion of normality for one night.

The fiends had stolen so much from me. I deserved a

chance to be *completely* free for them, if only for a brief moment before my responsibilities called once more.

Unfortunately, John had clearly been thinking about my early years too. He shifted to my other foot automatically, but his expression went serious, his mind on something other than my appendage.

"You lived in one of those communes for fourteen years, you said."

I nodded. To fill in the most essential blanks in their understanding, I'd told the trio the basic details of my history over the week when I'd been recovering.

"I can see why you needed to build up a certain amount of wealth and influence so that you'd be able to take on these creatures," he went on. I hadn't mentioned Olivia at all, but the scenes they'd witnessed in that other commune had shown them plenty of motivation for anyone to want to put an end to the shrouded folk's reign. "Why is it that you took the criminal route? Why not put your skills toward a legitimate business?"

His tone didn't reveal any judgment of my chosen line of work, but knowing John, the fact of it niggled at him. He was, really, the most *good* of the trio, his adrenaline junkie tendencies aside. The three of them all had their own motivations for coming to their lines of work. Sherlock liked to solve puzzles. Garrett had something to prove.

John... He cared about people, pure and simple. Which I supposed was an excellent quality for a doctor to have, and often useful for a consulting detective's partner as well, but it also meant he cared about all the people I'd conned over the years.

A little tension wound back through my gut. I ignored

it. I could give him an honest and reasonably complete answer.

"Growing up in a place like that," I said, "everything was out of our control. The adults pushed us into our various sacrifices and spats with each other. The shrouded folk directed the adults. I never even knew what the supposed 'high honor' I was competing for was until I snuck out to watch one of the older kids taken…" A shiver ran down my back at the memory of the blaze of light, the awful screams that had seemed to go on forever.

Sherlock was watching me intently now, but John's hand paused against my foot. "If you'd rather not talk about it—if it's too painful—"

I waved off his concern. "I can manage my own discomfort. I don't resent the question. Anyway, fourteen years of that left me with a deep need for control. I function best when I can direct as many pieces of a scheme as possible by my own will."

"And how does that need interfere with having a legitimate business that you own and operate yourself?"

I gave him a pointed look. "How do you think? Any completely legal way of making money involves all sorts of permissions and restrictions from outside parties—people I don't trust not to screw me over. If you want full control, it's easiest to simply ignore the law completely."

"Easiest for the perpetrator," Sherlock said wryly. "Not so much the victims."

My gaze shifted to him, the twinge I'd felt earlier digging more sharply into my chest. "I'm not going to tell you about all the things I've done, because I don't think you'd enjoy hearing them. But I hope you know me well enough by now to be able to 'deduce' that I don't hurt people for some sick enjoyment but only when it's necessary—and generally only those who have it coming. If I can rid this world of the shrouded folk, then I'll have ended a lot more misery than I've ever caused."

John started to rub my foot again with a gentle pressure. He spoke quietly, like an apology. "It's amazing that you made it through the childhood you had as strong as you are. I realize I can't really know what it was like, and I can't say what I might have felt I needed to do if I'd gone through the same thing."

I accepted that sentiment, but I didn't want to dwell on the past anymore. I wanted to get back to that warm, contented moment of a few minutes ago when it'd almost seemed that past had never existed. With a shove against the cushions and a bend of my knees, I scooted closer to him. "So, you're not going to chuck me out the door just yet, then?"

I'd never seen anything quite like the eagerly kind smile John Watson could produce, as bright as his blond hair. "I know you wouldn't hurt us."

He said it like a simple statement of fact when really it was all faith. My throat tightened at the words. Garrett had felt plenty hurt by the way I'd deceived him when we'd first met. During that early scheme, I could have ruined all of their careers if I'd wanted to—that had been my original plan.

But then, maybe I'd earned a bit of John's faith after all. I *had* changed my plans once I'd gotten to know the trio face to face. I'd saved their lives later on when Bash had come to my rescue, ready to set his gun blazing.

"No, I wouldn't," I said, bringing my fingers to his cheek. There was one thing I could get from these men that topped every other enjoyment I'd had tonight. "I have much better things to do with you."

I slipped my foot out of his grasp so I could lean the rest of the way to kiss him. He moved to meet me, one hand coming to rest on my waist as if to steady me—as if I needed steadying. As soon as our mouths collided, a rush of heat and assurance swept through me.

I wouldn't have these men forever. I might not even have them for the entirety of my mission. But damn, they did spark something deep during the time they were around. Right now, I wanted to take all the bliss of this sensation and see how high I could fan the flames, as if they might burn away everything awful in my life.

John kissed me tenderly and then with more passion, his other hand coming up to tangle in my hair. I devoured the sweetness of his mouth. He paused for a second, keeping his head close to mine, and glanced toward Sherlock as if in question.

The other man's posture had stiffened, but I recognized the hungry light in the back of Sherlock's eyes. Hunger both of us could provoke, it turned out. But the consulting detective didn't like to give in to carnal impulses simply for the sake of it. I could give him an excuse to justify the idea.

"I think we deserve a reward after the first part of the job well done," I said with a sly smile. "To clarify our thoughts for the rest to come, from tomorrow onward?"

He wet his lips, and I tracked the movement with another flash of heat. Then he got up without a word, set his pipe on the end table, and came to sit on the sofa at my other side. He traced the curve of my hip, and John pulled me into another kiss, and oh yes, this was bliss, all right. A joy no shrouded one could possibly conquer. The fiends wouldn't have had the slightest clue what to make of this encounter or what the purpose of it could possibly be.

Sherlock eased my hair to the side and kissed my neck, finding the sensitive spot he'd discovered I responded to well before. I growled at the bolt of pleasure that intensified with the nip of his teeth.

My fingers trailed down John's broad chest, and he teased his thumb over the peak of my breast. Sherlock dipped his hand right between my legs. My breath stuttered as he trailed it along my inner thigh to the spot that burned for contact. His lips seared a path of their own to the crook of my shoulder.

I kissed John long and hard, and then I nudged him back just far enough to allow me to speak. "I think we should take this to a bed. The only question is which one."

"Sherlock's," John said with a breathless laugh. "Much less of a mess."

Sherlock looked as if he might object to the mess *we* might end up making there, but when I caressed his lean torso through his linen shirt, desire overcame any resistance in his expression. "What are we waiting for, then?" he said matter-of-factly.

Having seen the way he kept his hotel rooms, I knew what to expect from Sherlock's bedroom, but walking into a place so entirely *him* still sent a happy quiver through me. Everything from the bedcovers to the books on the shelves along one wall was perfectly orderly, as John had suggested. The smoky tang of his pipe smoke lingered in the air.

John looked affected by it too. His pupils dilated, and he rested a tentative hand on his friend's shoulder. Sherlock glanced at him. Some silent communication seemed to pass between them before Sherlock leaned in and captured John's mouth with his own.

They kept touching me as they kissed each other,

John's hand on my back and Sherlock's on my hip. I simply watched the pleasure they took from each other for a moment, and then added to it by grazing my lips against Sherlock's skin just below his ear.

A few weeks ago, Sherlock had barely been able to admit his attraction to his long-time friend. Now, the two of them getting intimate looked as natural as breathing. Maybe I had hurt them in little ways before we'd gotten to this point, but I'd given them that gift too, hadn't I?

Sherlock pulled away from John to kiss me next. As he claimed my lips, John eased his hand up under my blouse. He loosened my bra. A moan slipped from my throat as he stroked my bare breast, sending a wash of giddy sensation through me.

Sherlock took the opportunity to kiss me even more deeply, taking the initiative with his tongue this time. I grasped the fly of his pants and yanked. The first couple times we'd come together like this, it'd been a slowly building seduction. Tonight I was ready to get to the best parts fast.

I pushed Sherlock onto the bed, tugging John with us too. His leg would bother him if he was standing for long without support. As he clambered onto the covers after me, the good doctor lifted my blouse right up over my head. Sherlock reached for the clasp of my pants, and I yanked his down. He cupped me through my panties with a skillful precision that brought a gasp to my lips. A hunger for even more flared all through my body.

As Sherlock and I kissed again, John brought his mouth to my breast. I nearly bit Sherlock's lip at the jolt of pleasure. I shifted my attention from one man to the other, stripping John of his collared shirt. While I claimed his mouth in turn, Sherlock fondled my breasts from behind, circling both nipples deftly and flicking his thumbs over them with little jolts of pleasure.

I dawdled on that bliss for a minute, kissing John as thoroughly as I was capable of. Then I swiveled and gave Sherlock a light shove as I kicked my pants the rest of the way off. He sank back on the bed, his long cock standing rigid at attention. My sex throbbed at the sight of it. I stroked the velvety skin from base to head, rewarded by the hitch of his chest.

"I need you inside me *now*."

Sherlock's eyes gleamed with a delight he couldn't hide. John pitched in by divesting me of my panties while I ripped open the condom packet I'd grabbed from my purse. I worked Sherlock over a few more times, slicking precum down his length. The second after I'd prepared him, I straddled him and sank down onto him, my eyes rolling back with the fresh burn of bliss.

John sprawled beside us, fondling my breast with one hand. I meant to urge him up the bed so I could take him in my mouth while I rode his friend, but at the same moment, Sherlock reached toward the other man. As I rose and eased down again over him, he traced the lines of John's chest tentatively. His gaze stayed fixed on his companion's face as if waiting for some sort of rejection.

John simply gazed back at him, a flush seeping up his neck and onto his cheeks.

Somewhere in our eager groping, I'd undone the fly of John's pants, even if I hadn't managed to get them off. Sherlock's hand hesitated at his friend's waist. His throat bobbed with an audible swallow. "John," he said in his overly formal way, "I would— That is, if you—"

"Yes," John said softly.

I stilled over Sherlock as he dipped his hand inside

John's pants. John closed his eyes, his lips parting. His expression was so ecstatic I practically came just watching him.

He rolled farther onto his side toward us. Sherlock began a careful but steady pumping. His gaze came back to me, and I bent down to kiss him, hoping I could convey just how very okay I was with this mutual adoration-fest. I caressed John's side, and he resumed his attentions to my breast, even as his hips started to twitch with the rhythm of Sherlock's helping hand.

I couldn't bear to stay still any longer. I started to ride Sherlock again, and he rolled his hips to meet me, filling me even deeper than I'd managed on my own. He gripped my thigh with his free hand, shifting his position slightly beneath me, and his cock hit a spot deep inside that sent pleasure pulsing through every part of my body. I couldn't hold in a whimper.

"There?" Sherlock said, sounding both eager and self-satisfied. He bucked to meet me, and I trembled with the sensation.

"Fuck, yes," was all I managed to reply. I rocked over him faster, and his hand on John sped up at the same time. We all moved together, sparking pleasure between the three of us in a weird unity that was nonetheless the most wonderful thing I'd ever experienced.

"Christ, Sherlock," John said in a strained voice, so clearly close to the edge that the words sent me tumbling right over. As Sherlock plunged into me, I cried out with the burst of my orgasm through my core. John groaned as he followed me. I kept bobbing up and down over Sherlock in my blissful haze until his grip on my thigh tightened. He came with a choked sound.

We collapsed into a warm, gleefully sweaty heap of

limbs. As I nestled there between the two men who should have been my enemies, an odd sense of peace spread through my chest.

I didn't know if I'd ever feel actual love in my life, for someone else or from them to me, but just now, in this moment, I caught a glimmer of what it might be like.

CHAPTER NINE

Bash

An engine roared beneath me, and dust kicked up in clouds beyond the open back of the army truck. Jemma's trio of London crime-fighters closed in around me, all of them decked out in full military fatigues.

Garrett grabbed my arm where I was sitting on the bench and wrenched me up so hard my shoulder nearly popped from its socket. I moved to resist, and my wrists jarred against a binding that bit into my skin. When I drew in a breath, the air crackled into my mouth, dry and gritty.

"Out you go!" Sherlock hollered, and pushed me toward the open door. "We don't need your kind around here."

John smacked his walking stick across my face. As my head spun, he shoved me even closer to the edge. "People like you don't deserve anything."

"Get the hell out of our lives!" Garrett snapped.

I tried to throw myself farther into the truck, and they

all heaved at me at the same time. I stumbled over the edge. The sensation of falling only lasted one lurching second before my head smacked into the hard-packed earth with an explosion of pain that—

I flinched awake in my bed. My heart thumped on and I could have sworn a dull ache lingered, creeping through the side of my head, but I wasn't in Afghanistan. I was in the bedroom of the temporary apartment I'd rented near Baker St. The plain white ceiling loomed over me as I swallowed to clear the taste of sand from my mouth.

Of course I was in my apartment in London. I'd left Afghanistan and the army nearly nine years ago. Jemma's trio had never been over there in the first place. It'd been a dream—a stupidly unsettling dream that I still couldn't quite shake the memory off as I got up and went to take a shower.

It might have been a dream, but it hadn't been entirely inaccurate, had it? Those three would have tossed me out of Jemma's mission in an instant if they could. I didn't figure any of them would forget the moment in Split when I'd been a twitch of my trigger finger away from killing the bunch of them.

I *had* been the one who'd invited them back into our lives, if only to save Jemma's. Maybe I should have killed them back then and spared us all the trouble. Jemma had charmed them, but in their eyes I was only the hired help, and a thug on top of that.

Jemma had offered to get me a rental in the same place she was staying, but I'd wanted to stay close to the main two in the trio in case this alliance went sour. The upside was it only took me five minutes to get from the apartment to Sherlock and John's for our planned morning meeting.

John was the one who answered the door. He smiled at me like he seemed to smile at just about everybody, but the expression he aimed at me didn't have quite the same warmth. The image flashed through my mind of his face in my dream, lip curled with disgust. I blinked it away, dipped my head to him, and came in without bothering with greetings.

Despite my close proximity, I was the last one to show up. The others were already sitting around the dining table, Jemma tucked in between Sherlock and Garrett, her hand brushing Garrett's arm as the cop said something she chuckled at. For all her cool collectedness, *she* had plenty of warmth for all three men now. As if Detective Inspector Lestrade wouldn't just have soon have seen all of the rest of us out of the picture so he could have her to himself.

The thought came with an uncomfortable prickling. As I took my seat, I exhaled, willing myself to focus.

Jemma flashed me a grin. "Right on time. Let's get started." She gave Garrett's shoulder a light poke. "You've been following up on the local investigation in the aftermath of the raid on the Lake District commune, haven't you?"

"Of course," the slight man said, his chin coming up. "A lot of horrifying stuff, as we'd all have expected. There was one kid they found in a hollowed-out room under one of the cabins…" His mouth twisted. "Anyway, these people don't seem to keep a whole lot of written records, but the local department turned up a few things that might point us in the right direction. At least I hope so, considering the hassle my own coworkers are giving me over my interest in the case."

"Does it bother them that you're following up?" Sherlock said with a frown. "Surely they can understand why you'd check in, what with my own involvement and your key role in directing the investigation?"

Garrett tossed up his hands in an unexpectedly violent motion. "I don't know what goes through their heads. Most likely their heads are all full of rocks, the way they go around. More interested in gossip than actually getting any work done. They're all bloody useless fuckers."

There was a momentary silence around the table as we all hesitated. The cop had a temper, but he didn't usually shoot off his mouth to that extent out of the blue. Jemma peered at Garrett, knitting her brow. "Did something particularly bad happen when you were at work yesterday?"

The man rubbed his mouth, his expression still tight, his posture defensive. "No. I just—I get sick of them. That's all. Nothing so strange about that. You hear the way Sherlock talks about them."

The explanation didn't ring totally true to me, but I didn't really give a shit what bee the cop had in his bonnet anyway. "What's the useful evidence you got?" I said. "That's the important part." Not his petty grievances.

Garrett shot me a look as if he were going to snap at me too, but his voice came out even enough now. "They found some sort of order invoice with an address that just led to a farm down near Dover. They left it at that, but the data we got together earlier suggests there's been other activity in that general area. This address completes a sort of ring that I'd expect a commune or similar is sitting in the middle of. Not a very large one, though, from the level of activity."

"That's a start," John said briskly. He drummed his hands on the edge of the table. "We can pursue that."

"Is that all?" Sherlock asked. "As enjoyable as your

enthusiasm is, my dear Watson, I think we should hear all the possibilities before leaping ahead."

Garrett shook his head. "On top of that, they found items they were able to determine came from a couple areas in the Scottish Highlands. Also near some points of activity we observed earlier—a little more there. Although it's been harder to get clear data because the departments in Scotland aren't always so keen on cooperating with London… I'm planning on doing some further digging as I can."

"It sounds like there must be some association between the different communes here," Jemma said with a cock of her head. "I don't remember mine being in communication with other settlements, but then, at my age, they probably wouldn't have shared that kind of information with me. It'd certainty help with ensuring all the nearby communes had enough supplies and support if they ran into trouble."

"The Highlands location has shown evidence of being a larger target," Sherlock said. "Why don't we continue our own investigations from a distance and see what we come up with in a few days' time before taking any more direct steps?"

John looked at him, his hand still shifting restlessly. "Can we really afford to wait? The crimes they're committing on a regular basis…"

"We need to be fully prepared," Sherlock said firmly. "We can't afford to step wrong and throw the whole operation against this menace off."

"The place in Dover isn't that far from here," Garrett said. "It wouldn't be difficult to scout out more closely."

"If we're going to look more closely, I say we go straight to the bigger commune," John said.

Sherlock raised his eyebrows. "We don't even know for certain that it *is* larger. I'd say—"

A tension I hadn't fully registered building inside me suddenly overflowed. I smacked my hands down on the table. "I say you all shut up and let's get something done. What the hell is the point of all this arguing?"

Sherlock stiffened. "Determining the best course of action is an essential part of any—"

"Not when you're going in circles. Here's a simple plan: We investigate everything and every way we can investigate. That matters more than any of you being 'right' or whatever you're trying to prove."

"Bash," Jemma said quietly, and my gaze jerked to her. She was watching me much the same way she'd looked at Garrett a few minutes ago, her forehead lightly furrowed, concern shining in her blue-gray eyes. As the prickle of frustration eased off, I realized I'd just said more in the space of a minute than I'd generally contributed to these discussions at all. I let the rest of them do their talking, and then I carried out what Jemma needed doing. That was my role.

They just were getting on my nerves today.

Jemma's intervention cooled my jets, though. I let out a huff of breath. "Do what you want," I said to the others. "But what I said stands."

"I would like to take some actual action," John said, glancing around the table. "I suppose Dover *is* closer… It couldn't hurt to go out and take a careful scope around the area today, could it?"

Yes. Let's get away from this table and their constant discussion and crack a few heads. "I'll go with you," I said. "Strength in numbers. And I know enough to make sure you don't screw everything up."

I looked to Jemma again, wondering if she'd insist on joining us, but she simply nodded. Maybe she was glad to see me outright offering to collaborate with one of her trio.

"Let me quickly go over all the information we already have on that spot and see if I have any pointers," she said. "Then it's all yours."

"Not so much a ring as a semi-circle," John said, studying the map. He'd made a similar comment earlier in the drive, but at least when he was talking he wasn't moving about restlessly in the passenger seat. Maybe I'd let him drive on the way back. I'd preferred to have primary control over our route, but it might be worth the trade-off to have him fully occupied.

"That still makes it easy to narrow down where the place might be," I said. The data the trio had gathered from their various sources pointed us to a section of the country's southern coastline, high up on a cliff over the sea. Jemma's cult did have a thing for elevation. "How much farther to that farm now?"

"Ten miles. How close do you think we should go to the likely area?"

"Close enough to see where the edge of their surveillance is. That's the most important factor if we're going to crash their party."

John nodded with a knowing expression. "Any facility's security is only as good as the men on guard." He paused. "Or women, I suppose. We didn't have many of those in our unit in Iraq, so sometimes my phrasing is a little skewed."

I glanced away from the road to briefly study his face. I'd known John had been in the field overseas from Jemma's preliminary research on the Londoners, but there was so little military in his demeanor I hadn't thought about it in a while. Beneath that apparently soft exterior was a man who'd endured a similar environment to the one I had. It could be that the only reason he wasn't still out there was the blast that had left him needing that walking stick.

"Do you regret joining the service?" I asked abruptly. "If you hadn't, you'd still be a surgeon, right?"

John blinked at me. He might not realize just how much intel Jemma had shared. "No," he said after a moment, with what sounded like honest thoughtfulness. "And not just because I'm very happy with the career I have now. Going over there gave me a sense of a higher purpose on a broader level that I hadn't really felt before. I'm glad I have that, however I'm going to apply it." He smiled. "And it's always good to test your limits and discover how much you can survive."

I had to chuckle at that. "No kidding."

I returned my focus to the road, but I felt him studying me in turn. "Where were you stationed?" he ventured.

Was he guessing or had Jemma mentioned my time in the army? I guessed it didn't matter for him to know. "Afghanistan. Pretty brutal. I don't regret going either, because of the things it taught me about myself and everyone else, but I sure as hell wouldn't go back."

"No. I think once is enough."

The set of John's mouth resonated with something inside me. As huge a distance as there was between me and the three of them, he and I at least had more common understanding than I'd considered. I didn't want to be best pals with the guy, but the prickly sensation that had lingered since my dream eased with a touch of warmth.

He might have overly grandiose ideas about good and evil, but John Watson was okay. He'd gotten his hands dirty—he'd put in the work.

He shifted in his seat. "Here's the farm. Take a right at the crossroad."

I followed his directions, easing up on the gas with each passing mile, until the road turned into a dirt track and a metal gate came into view another half a mile up ahead. At the sight of it, I pulled the car over to the side of the road.

The track led on past the gate across a short stretch of field and then on into hilly woodland. The cult liked the cover of forests as much as they liked to be high above sea level. I scanned the area but didn't see any sign of security other than that gate. There might not even be a commune beyond it—it could be another farm or country property for all we knew.

"Should we go on foot from here?" John asked.

"I think that makes the most sense." I shoved open the door. "Better make it look like we're wandering tourists in case anyone's watching from the woods. If they don't want us to get that close, they'll turn us back quickly enough, and that'll tell us something right there."

I had to admit that John knew how to play a part well when he needed to. He got out of the car with that entitled vacationer air already in place, giving his walking stick a quick whirl. We approached the gate without incident. A padlock hung from the chain that held it closed, so I clambered over and helped John follow me.

We ambled along as if sightseeing until we reached the

cover of the forest. No one stepped out to shoo us away. I started scanning our surroundings more warily, watching for any human movement or other sign of habitation. John shifted the branches of a shrub with his stick here, peered down at the dirt track there. The third time he knelt down, he stayed there.

"Someone drove through here recently?"

I crouched across from him. "How can you tell?"

He motioned to a tiny blotch in the dirt. "Oil. Still on the surface, not quite dry yet. Sherlock probably could have given you an accurate estimate to the hour—the best I can say is I think it couldn't have been more than a day ago they went through. It doesn't tell us a lot, but there's obviously someone who's been active out this way."

I straightened up. "Let's see if we can find out what they've been up to."

John spotted a few more specks of oil as we walked on. Birds chattered in the trees, and the warm summer breeze erased any coolness the shadows might have provided. We'd been on the trail maybe an hour without encountering anyone or anything human-made when a hint of a scent reached my nose. I stopped in my tracks.

"Do you smell that?" I said quietly.

John had come to a halt when I had. He took a breath, and his eyebrows rose. "Smoke," he said. "Not just ordinary wood smoke either. Something's been burning that wasn't meant to be burnt."

Yes, I'd caught the chemical flavor to the smoke too. My nerves on edge, I set off again a little faster than before. Something about this whole situation didn't feel right.

The smell thickened as we hurried on. The track came to an abrupt end—and we found ourselves looking at what I assumed had once been a garage, now nothing more than a few pieces of charred walls and a heap of burnt rubble.

"What the hell happened here?" John said under his breath. "Do these people have enemies other than Jemma?"

"Not that she's ever mentioned to me. And I'm sure she would have made use of them if they existed." I peered between the trees and thought I made out a dark shape up ahead that wasn't a tree. "Come on."

We crept along cautiously at first and then with more confidence as it became clear no one at all was left in this godforsaken place. Eight cabins scattered the woods about a mile from the garage, but all of them had been burned, roofs crumbled, innards hollowed out, what remained of the wooden walls little more than cinders. Many of the trees near them were charred as well. I wouldn't be surprised if the only reason there hadn't been a huge forest fire was the recent rains.

The smoky stench hung thick in the air here. A huge pile of ash with no sign of walls or anything to mark it as a building lay in the approximate middle of the settlement. I walked up to it and poked it with a broken branch I picked up, sifting through fragments of blackened paper and melted bits of plastic. Understanding rose up inside me.

"This wasn't something some enemy did to them. They did it to themselves. They were getting rid of evidence. This must have been the stuff they particularly wanted to destroy."

John let out a low whistle. "Do you think they heard about the raid and figured they might be next?"

"Who knows? These people are insane, and I'm not

sure the creatures that direct them are any less crazy." I dug deeper into the pile of ash, hoping I might find some shred of evidence to bring back to Jemma, but they'd done a thorough job. The chemical smell was at least partly kerosene, I recognized now. The stuff had been doused to make sure it burned. Probably the buildings had been too.

"We check all the cabins," I said. "Grab anything that's got any kind of identifying mark on it, any text, anything we might be able to get information out of. Jemma won't be happy if we lose this bunch completely."

Jemma

The woman behind the reception desk gave the four of us a bemused look. "What are you here about again?"

"The parent company hired us to take a look at your computer security systems," Sherlock said in a clipped voice that didn't sound at all like his own. "All we need is a station with internet capability, ideally in an office we can have to ourselves for the hour or so the testing will take. I have the work order right here."

He produced a paper I'd had one of my many contacts in the forging business put together for us. The receptionist glanced at it and then at us again.

We'd gone for the most clear computer-geek stereotypes, all of us in one sort of glasses or another, slacks and plain button-up shirts, my bright hair hidden under a much dowdier wig. The only one who stuck out a bit was Sherlock's Irregular addition to our crew—a girl named Marissa who couldn't have been more than eighteen but who apparently could hack circles around just about anyone. But she mustn't have looked ridiculously young, because the receptionist picked up her phone.

"Let me see what I can do," she said, and five minutes later one of the staff escorted us into a small but private room with a few desks and a couple of laptops.

"Is there anything else you need?" the guy said.

"I think we're good to go," John replied, keeping his own voice flatter than usual. None of us wanted to be recognized if we had to make another appearance here in a more official capacity. Not that I expected that would be very likely.

The guy left, I locked the door behind him, and Marissa dropped into a chair in front of one of the computers with a crack of her knuckles. "Give me five, maybe ten minutes," she said, her gaze already intent on the screen. "I'll have it all laid out for you by then."

"We'll leave you to it," Sherlock said in his usual dry tone.

The three of us wandered through the room while Marissa's fingers clattered over the keys. The florescent light overhead gave off a faint buzzing, and the air had a lemony waxy smell as if someone had recently polished the floor, but I'd been in worse spots.

John leaned against the far end of the table. He lowered his voice so as not to disturb Marissa's work. "We're only looking for the details of a theft, right?"

"If it even exists." I fished in my purse for the pen that had been among the seemingly random assortment of items he and Bash had brought back from the burnt-out commune near Dover. The tip was scorched and the body partly melted, but not so much that we hadn't been able to make out the company logo printed on the side: Havenboard Foods. The business stocked a variety of grocery and corner stores throughout southern England.

Sherlock nodded. "There are many ways that pen could have ended up in the commune other than by the theft of a shipment. Businesses give out promotional materials of that sort in large quantities. It'd have been easy enough for a cultist who temporarily left the settlement to happen to pick one up any number of places."

He spoke evenly, but his expression was darker than usual. A bit of a cloud had been hanging over him since we'd rounded up the group this morning. I hadn't seen him in one of his morose moods since that first week we'd spent together when he'd been temporarily stumped by the case I'd presented the trio with.

It didn't make sense for him to be withdrawing in frustration now. We had plenty of leads and had hardly exhausted any of them.

"Have any other cases come up while you've been working on this?" I asked, taking a roundabout route to getting at my real question. Sherlock had ego to spare. If I suggested that he was behaving irrationally or overly affected by emotion, his kneejerk reaction would be denial.

He gave me a look that was almost a glower. "Don't worry, all my attention has been on these operations."

I was a little stung by his assumption that I'd meant to question his dedication. "That wasn't the point I was getting at. You seem... more preoccupied than usual this morning, and I wondered why."

"I'm merely eager to gather more information so that we can arrive at clearer conclusions," Sherlock said.

Eager wasn't at all the word I'd have used to describe his demeanor. Apparently Watson was on my side. "Perhaps we both had a restless night," he said in his gentle way. "Everything we've seen and had to think about involving these creatures—it can stick in the mind in unfortunate ways. I had a couple of horrible dreams." He grimaced and rubbed his forehead as if he could wipe them from his mind that way.

Sherlock snorted. "We're in a sorry state if we let mental flights of fancy distract us from our cause. Let's keep our focus on what's real, shall we?"

The reprimand came out sharp rather than teasing—enough so that John winced. I frowned, eyeing the consulting detective. I might be wrong, but I thought I detected a whiff of "thou doust protest too much" in that abrupt dismissal. Perhaps Sherlock *had* been troubled by bad dreams too, and it was irritating him that he was bothered at all.

Something troublesome had clearly gotten into the air lately. Garrett and Bash had both seemed more hot-tempered than usual the last few days. Garrett had gotten outright cruel in some of the comments he'd made about his colleagues, and Bash... I'd never seen Bash come anywhere near losing his cool, so even the small hints of temper he'd shown made me concerned.

I'd managed to stay in Sherlock's presence, or at least no more than a room or two away from him, for most of the time since the shrouded one had marked him, and I hadn't detected any of them nearby since then. Had one of them gotten to him—to all of them—somehow anyway? My stomach twisted at the thought.

It could very well be simply the stress of our current mission. I had to remember that the shrouded folk had been an undeniable part of my reality for my entire life. These men had only just been introduced to the idea of monsters far beyond anything they'd have considered possible. They'd witnessed horrors and seen evidence of more beyond that. I'd told them terrifying stories.

They might be experts in their fields, but nothing could have prepared them to face an enemy like this. I'd just keep an eye on them in case the emotional fraying appeared to get any worse.

John started pacing again. His mood had stayed warm and enthusiastic as usual, but he'd definitely been restless. Now he grabbed a chair by the other laptop in the room and flipped the computer open with a click to peer at the screen. "Maybe I can do some digging too."

"I think it's rather better if you didn't, John," Sherlock said, confusion as well as alarm crossing his face. "You don't have the best track record with computing devices, as I recall. I'm sure Marissa can handle it without leaving any traces that might come back to haunt us… so to speak."

John let out an impatient huff. "I just—"

"I'm in!" Marissa chirped, stirring us all into action. John sprang up, and we hustled around the table to look at the hacker's screen.

I knew my way around a computer, but not on the level this girl obviously did. The various windows with their lists of text didn't mean a whole lot to me. Marissa looked up at Sherlock. "What do you want me to bring up first?"

"Financial records," he said quickly, intentness focusing his gaze and wiping away some of his earlier melancholy. "We want to see if they had to compensate for a missing shipment any time in the last several years—and if so, exactly what and when."

Our hope was, if the pen had gotten to the commune via a theft, that we'd learn more about the commune's habits from the details around that theft. I didn't like the fact that they'd slipped out of our grasp so easily. If we could figure out their usual area of activity, where they might have gone from their original settlement…

"Let's see," Marissa murmured to herself, her hands flying over the keyboard again. "Here, these look like the right set of statements. What kind of numbers do you think we'd be looking for?"

"Fairly large, in the thousands of dollars at least," Sherlock said. "And the same value twice close together—one shipment dispatched that never reached it's intended destination, and a matching one put together shortly after."

"On it." She opened up another window and typed something into that, and the spreadsheets of data started whipping through the rows of their own accord. She paused a couple of times on spots that looked like a possibility, but one turned out to be an identical order for two different stores, and another was a swift restocking after the initial order must have immediately run out, with full payment for both.

"That's five years," Marissa said after several minutes of scanning. "Do you want me to keep going back?"

John shifted his weight, standing at a bit of an angle to reduce the pressure on his weaker leg since he hadn't brought his walking stick. "There might not be anything. This could be all a red herring."

"We told them we'd be here an hour," I said. "We

might as well make use of it. Who knows when that pen was last used. Let's try another five, just in case."

Sherlock motioned for Marissa to continue, and I let my eyes linger on the screen as she continued her search. A word jumped out at me that made my pulse stutter.

"Stop!" I said, grabbing her shoulder.

Marissa stiffened, and I immediately let go, but she'd halted the search. "What?" she said.

"Go back up. Slower this time. I saw something."

"What was it, Jemma?" John asked.

"Just—let me make sure."

The entry came into view. "There," I said. "Leave it there." I pointed to the line, my heart still thumping faster than before. In the column that labeled the sources of the payments or expenses, that row simply said SHROUD.

John drew in a startled breath. Sherlock leaned closer, his eyebrows drawing together. "You don't think— A regular company wouldn't be doing *business* with this cult, would they?"

"I don't know. I wouldn't have thought so. I've never seen it happen before, but I've been pretty out of the loop since I left." I rubbed my mouth, still staring at the line. It was an expense—something provided to SHROUD from Havenboard Foods. "Are there any stores or other companies with a name that includes 'Shroud' they might have been dealing with?"

Marissa opened an internet search window in a flash. "I don't see anything like that," she said after a moment.

"I've never heard of one," Sherlock added. "But it could have some other meaning."

It could. Why on earth would this company be giving anything to the cult? What would they have been giving it in exchange for?

I wet my lips. "We might be able to get a better idea. Search and see if any other expenses like that come up."

Marissa tapped the keys. In a matter of seconds, another item came up, from about six months later. Then six months after that. Regular intervals, all the way up to a few months ago. My chest had constricted. I pulled out my phone. "I'm going to check those dates."

I looked up one and then another and then a third, my stomach sinking farther with each confirmation. After five, I decided I had proof enough.

"It's them," I said. "I don't know why, but this company has some kind of an association set up with the cult."

"Would they really label it so plainly?" Sherlock protested.

I raised my eyebrows at him. "Who would it be plain to? Other than the members of the cult, the five of us are the only people who know the shrouded folk even exist. Well, us and whoever decided on that label, apparently. What better way to keep it secret than to use a name no one knows about?"

"It could be a coincidence," John ventured, but he looked uncertain.

I shook my head and waved my phone. "All of the deliveries or payments or whatever Havenboard provided were made on the dates of the full moon. That's when the cult prefers to arrange any business where they have to involve outsiders. The folk can stay more active on the brightest nights—the commune would want to have them around for protection as need be."

Silence filled the room for a moment. Sherlock's jaw worked. "It seems this situation is even more complex than you anticipated."

I swallowed hard. "Yes. Apparently it's not just the cult and the folk we have to contend with. They have at least one real ally in the wider world as well. And someone with enough clout that they could arrange these expenses without any questions being asked."

Jemma

"I just had eyes on the meeting," Bash said through my earpiece. "They're still jabbering away."

Sitting next to me in the car, Sherlock raised his eyebrows in question. I shook my head and pressed the button on my mic to reply to Bash. "Keep watching them and let me know as soon as they look like they're getting up."

"Aye, aye, Majesty."

A smile touched my lips at the fond if teasing nickname.

Sherlock gazed out the window at the brick building across the street where MP Harvey Tillhouse had his office. His hands were clasped tightly together in his lap, and a shadow crossed his face. The moroseness I'd noticed in him at Havenboard hadn't lifted.

He turned back to me with a slight jerk of his arm. "This fellow is a talkative one, isn't he?"

"I have no idea how long is normal with these strategy

meetings." I shrugged. "It doesn't matter. We'll be ready when he's leaving." We were decked out in new disguises —a blond wig for me and dun brown for Sherlock, colored contacts for both of us, a false beard straggling across his chin. I held a larger microphone on the seat next to me, ready for action, and Sherlock had a video camera with a doctored TV channel logo sitting on his lap.

My nonchalance didn't appear to alleviate Sherlock's gloom. He sighed and tipped his head against the headrest, his eyes going distant behind the bright brown lenses. His fingers squeezed tight enough around each other to turn his knuckles white.

I considered and decided to bite the bullet. It was just the two of us right now—he didn't have to feel he was admitting weakness to anyone else. We had time. And if my most brilliant crime fighter had a problem, I'd like to know about it sooner rather than later.

"What is it about this case that's bothering you?" I asked.

Sherlock's head snapped down and around. He studied me with a frown. "Who says it's bothering me?"

I rolled my eyes. "I know you well enough to see it. *Something* has been dragging at your mood. If it's not dealing with the shrouded folk, you can tell me what it is instead." I patted his leg, letting my hand linger just long enough to take the gesture from casual to flirtatious. "It's not as if I'm going to think there's anything odd about finding this whole thing difficult to take in."

For a second, Sherlock looked even grimmer. Then he let out another sigh. "I don't like cases where I can't get a sense of the full picture. There's too much about these creatures I can't fully comprehend—that I can only barely believe in the first place. And it certainly doesn't help that this latest development takes us beyond even your prior experience with the creatures."

"I can't say I'm particularly happy about that either." I made a face at the building across the street. We'd spent the last few days tracing various leads to try to figure out how Havenboard was connected to the shrouded folk. Our investigations had led us through a winding path of sign-offs and corporate shells to Tillhouse, a politician out of Yorkshire who owned the company that owned the company that owned Havenboard.

We'd determined that Havenboard's warehouse had been dropping off a large supply of nonperishable food and other supplies at a secluded storage building not far from the abandoned commune on a biannual basis. We'd also determined that the chain of commands to place that order had come from one of the few people with executive power over the company. Yesterday we'd eliminated the president of Havenboard from consideration. Now we were going to scope out Tillhouse.

"I suppose there are all sorts of benefits a politician planning on running for party leadership might get out of a paranormal ally," Sherlock said, following my gaze. Tillhouse might be only an MP now, but he was in the process of campaigning to take over as head of the Conservative Party. "The bigger surprise might be that it hasn't happened before."

"The shrouded folk don't like anyone outside their cult knowing about them," I said. "They expressly forbid revealing themselves to non-worshippers. How the hell this guy or anyone else in the company could have found out about them to even try to set up some sort of arrangement... I don't even know." All we'd been able to determine for sure was that the arrangement had been going on for nearly seven years.

"It won't matter anyway," I added. "We'll continue taking down the cult piece by piece, and there's nothing this guy can do about that. And when the cult's gone, the shrouded folk won't have the power left here to do anything for him. We just need to know who we're up against before we do anything else."

"Yes." Sherlock's solemn expression hadn't budged. He rolled his shoulders with a twitch of his neck, seeming to sink even deeper into the gloom in his head. Then, abruptly, he unclasped his hands and reached to touch my face. "Jemma?"

Even with the disguise hiding his familiar features, a flutter passed through my chest having this man train his gaze on me that intently. "Yes?"

He didn't say anything else, just drew me in for a kiss. A determined kiss, so hot it was dizzying coming out of nowhere like that. I didn't know what had gotten into him, but I wasn't going to pass up the opportunity to kiss him back just as enthusiastically.

Sherlock pulled back with a frown that wasn't at all the reaction I'd have wanted to provoke. "I thought perhaps— A different sort of stimulation— But I don't think that's the right route. I just need more answers."

"I don't know." I gave him a playful nudge. "Maybe we didn't try hard enough. You know I can offer plenty more 'stimulation' than just a kiss."

Even though he'd declared the kiss a failure, a faint flush of heat colored his skin at that remark. The sight of it lit a little fire in me. Unfortunately, this wasn't the time or place for any sort of deeper intimacy. As Bash helpfully reminded me with his voice carrying into my ear.

"They're getting up. That's your cue. Good luck!"

"Luck has nothing to do with it," I said smoothly, and shoved open the door.

Sherlock followed me out without needing any further prompting. We crossed the street and went down the alley to the building's back entrance. He already had his lockpicks in hand when we reached it. It took all of five seconds for him to force the deadbolt over.

If we'd gone in the front, the receptionist would have stopped us. This way, we slipped down the hall and up the staircase just in time to catch Tillhouse coming down the second-floor hall from the meeting room.

He looked like the kind of guy who *would* own companies that owned other companies. Square-jawed and flinty-eyed but with his silver hair slicked back in a posh style and his suit cut in the latest fashion. His staff flitted this way and that around him. One guy stopped beside him when Tillhouse stopped, the assistant giving us a cold look. "What's this about?"

I focused all my attention on the MP with a cajoling smile. "Mr. Tillhouse, we were just hoping to get a few comments on your suggested policy updates. It'll only take a minute or two. We'll give you the chance to review any clips before they air."

"I don't know how you got in here," the assistant started, but Tillhouse halted his complaint with a hand on his shoulder. He gave me a smarmy smile in return.

"I think we should reward ambition, don't you, Philip? All right. You have a minute or two. Everyone else, carry on with what you're supposed to be doing."

Any staff lingering in the hall dispersed. Sherlock raised his camera and started recording while I held up my microphone. I wanted the man's reactions on video so I could study them at my leisure afterward to make sure I hadn't missed anything—or to analyze what I did see in the moment more closely.

"You've said you'll campaign for legislation that allows more opportunities for businesses to expand without restriction," I said, jumping in with the talking points I'd prepared. "What sorts of checks and balances would you keep in place?"

I didn't really listen to his answer, only enough so that I'd be able to react if I needed to. Instead I watched his expression, his body language, checking for any of the tics only someone who'd spent years among the cult of the shrouded folk would have noticed. Nothing overt stood out, but he rubbed his forearm at one point when he paused to decide how to phrase part of his answer. The gesture caught my eye.

I asked another question, a faster one this time, and then I let out a light laugh. "And this may sound frivolous, but many of our viewers will be curious to know—you're always so well-dressed. What designer came up with this lovely suit?"

As I spoke, my hand shot out to give his sleeve a teasing tug. I angled it perfectly so I displaced the cuff of his shirt underneath as well. For just a second, I caught a glimpse of the skin of his inner wrist and an inch beyond. Skin with a tropical tan other than a thin slash of a paler mark. My stomach turned.

Anyone else would have taken that for a birthmark, no doubt, but I'd seen that shape, that shading before. Tillhouse had been exposed to a blast of the shrouded folk's power.

The MP pulled his arm away from me with an answering laugh, not seeming concerned about the contact. He didn't have any reason to think I'd recognize that mark any more than he must have thought anyone would figure out what SHROUD referred to.

"This one's Richard James," he said, and waved for Sherlock to turn off the camera. "All right, I think you got more than the time you asked for."

I would have been fine with the progress we'd already made, but as soon as Sherlock lowered the camera, Tillhouse leaned closer to me. He tapped the neckline of my dress where it lay a couple inches below my collarbone. "I don't think what I'm wearing is half as lovely as this, though."

Understanding flashed through me. He found me attractive. I'd wrapped plenty of men around my little finger using that advantage—I'd manipulated my London trio that way, among other strategies, when I'd first met them. Peek at him through my eyelashes, ease closer to him, exchange another touch or two, and I could have all his clothes off within an hour, I'd bet. Imagine how much I might find out then.

Those thoughts crossed my mind—and jarred against my awareness of Sherlock standing next to me. Something inside me balked.

Yes, I'd used sex as a tool to get my way dozens of times in the past, when it was the *only* way I'd known how to use it and any pleasurable parts were secondary. I knew what it was like to fuck with full passion now, to get off with a partner I cared about who cared about me. To treat the act like a ploy again, with this asshole who'd conspired with the shrouded folk somehow, made my very skin recoil.

I got ahold of myself within a second. Taking down the shrouded folk was worth *anything*. I sure as hell wasn't above a pragmatic fuck along the way. I forced a smile to my lips and started to speak, but my momentary resistance must have shown. Tillhouse was already pulling back from me, his demeanor cooling. I'd rejected him without even meaning to.

"I look forward to reviewing the segment," he said. "I trust you know the way out?"

"Yes," I said, suppressing my frustration with myself. "We can handle that."

I could still use that information later, I told myself as we went down to the main floor. I could catch him somewhere when we weren't on the job and make out as if my hesitation had been professional rather than personal. It wouldn't be that hard.

And yet my skin still shivered uncomfortably imagining it.

I'd gone fucking soft. That wasn't how my alliance with the trio was supposed to work. Damn it.

A woman was standing by the front door when we reached it. She beamed at us. "He's just wonderful, isn't he?"

"Absolutely," I said, beaming right back at her and willing her the hell out of our way.

"He's gaining so much ground already," she went on, a little breathless. "I'm sure he's going to get the leadership. Just think—in less than a year he could be prime minister of the whole country."

My inner turmoil quieted under a jolt of horror. Someday soon the man I'd just talked to might rule this entire country… while carrying a debt to the shrouded folk they were no doubt waiting to fully cash in on.

CHAPTER TWELVE

John

I came home from a grocery shopping trip to find Sherlock sitting in the living room drawing his bow across his violin. The sound of him playing—and playing a song I didn't recognize, which meant he was probably making it up on the spot—wasn't unusual, but as I slid a carton of eggs and a week's worth of vegetables into the fridge, my stomach started to tighten. There was a frenetic quality to the movement of the bow and the melody he was producing that wasn't all that usual.

I hadn't heard him play like that in over a year.

He didn't stop even when I closed the fridge and walked over to the sofa beside him. His hand kept whipping back and forth, and his eyes started straight ahead with a pinched alertness, the pupils dilated. A flush colored his cheeks. He hadn't left any paraphernalia out, but I didn't need to see the tools to know what he'd done with them.

I stepped right in front of him, so close that if he'd

shifted the violin an inch it'd have hit my gut. He slowed his strokes of the bow, his gaze flitting up to me now. The music quieted, but he still kept playing.

"Is my improvisation disturbing you, John?" he said in a breathless tone. I liked that voice when the enthusiasm in it came from the thrill of a case—or more intimate sorts of passion. Knowing any emotion it held today was artificial only made my stomach knot more.

"How much did you take?" I said, holding his gaze firmly.

"Oh, only a very moderate dosage. Don't worry yourself—I measured it carefully."

"You told me you weren't going to turn to the drug anymore."

He managed to make a dismissive motion of his shoulders without losing his rhythm. "I told you I'd hold off if it seemed unnecessary. I didn't promise to give the stuff up completely. Now and then my mind needs a good jolt to find the right track. We've discussed this."

We had, more than once, and I couldn't say I'd ever come away from those discussions completely satisfied. The idea that this genius of a man would insist on poisoning his brain and body with cocaine clashed with everything else I knew about him.

But there were certain other emotions, certain types of stillness and uncertainty, that he found it incredibly hard to tolerate. Even a genius had weaknesses. I'd just started to believe he was over this one.

"And have you made some additional progress under its influence?" I asked. If anything would convince him to leave off another injection, it'd be the logic he valued so highly. If the drug *didn't* help, why take it at all?

"My thoughts are much sharper now," Sherlock said.

"I *can* promise you that I know my limits. This was exactly what I needed."

He said that so matter-of-factly that I didn't know how to argue with him. How could I dispute the activity of his own mind or how he'd spurred it on? I had never been the brains between the two of us. My job was to support and provide a sounding board and occasionally whack a troublesome fellow or two with my walking stick.

Sherlock wasn't looking for guidance right now. He'd found it in a dissolved white powder.

I couldn't help trying anyway. "Is there any way I can help with your newfound clarity?"

Sherlock gave a brisk shake of his head. "I'm still sorting through the concepts as they come to me. I'm sure this will lead us to a productive route soon enough. You'll be the first to know."

He shot me a smile so bright I couldn't help smiling back, even as my throat tightened too. Damn the cocaine; damn Sherlock's enjoyment of it.

Knowing what was fueling his music, I couldn't stand to stay in the flat while he played on like that. I grasped my walking stick where I'd left it by the door.

"I'll leave you to it then."

He didn't even ask where I was off to now as I headed out.

Which might have been a good thing, because I didn't have the foggiest idea where I was going. I set off down the street with the urge to find something useful to do nagging at me. I could accomplish more than just waiting around for Sherlock to figure out how he needed me, couldn't I?

I just wasn't entirely sure what. I didn't have the sort of contacts who'd be able to share information about this MP who seemed tied up in the shrouded folk's business. All our focus had been on him since we'd discovered the connection.

Well, maybe Jemma could point me in a productive direction. I dug out my phone as I walked on, my walking stick tapping against the pavement with a sound much more decisive than anything else about me at the moment.

Evening was falling, pulling the shadows long and dimming the remaining daylight between them. The air pressed down, muggy beneath the thickening clouds gathering overhead.

Jemma picked up after just one ring. "What is it?" she said, and I realized she probably assumed this was some kind of emergency. I'd normally simply have texted her unless I had urgent news.

"Nothing's wrong," I said quickly. "I just—I'm out and about, and I wondered if there was anything you needed looking into."

The explanation sounded weak when I said it out loud. As if Jemma wouldn't have told me without being asked if she'd needed me for something. But I was talking to her now. At least the impression of her presence on the other end of the phone line kept my restlessness a little more at bay.

"I'm not sure there's anything I can delegate to you at the moment," she said, her voice turning a bit wry. "Are you getting bored?"

"Maybe a little. I'm not sure it's so much that." I veered right at the next intersection at random, pushing myself a little faster even though my hip twinged. Burning off the impatient energy might do the trick. "I haven't been of much use in general with the latest developments."

"You've helped plenty," Jemma said. "Who else would corral Sherlock half as well?"

She was partly teasing, but a jab shot through me all the same at the thought of how I'd failed to stop him from doing the thing I hated most just this evening. The words to tell her what he'd immersed himself in rose in my throat, but something—maybe the guilt of that failure, maybe the sense that it was Sherlock's business whether Jemma knew what he got up to—held them back.

"I guess I'll just have to hope our next lead takes more of a medical angle," I said, matching her tone. My gaze meandered along the street and came to an abrupt halt on the fence surrounding a construction site on the opposite side of the road.

Something flickered on the other side of the fence, visible only for a moment through the chain-link gate. A piece of paper blown in the breeze, I thought. And I could have sworn I'd seen Harvey Tillhouse's photograph printed on it.

What did he have to do with whatever they were building over there?

"John?" Jemma said as I crossed the street, in a tone that suggested I'd missed something she'd said earlier.

"I think I might have a lead right here," I said. "I'll let you know if it pans out. I think I'd better get off the phone so I can take a real look."

"Take a real look? What are you doing?"

"Nothing I can't handle." I peered through the gate at the jumble of wood and steel heaped around the pit that I supposed was going to be a building's basement. The frame rose up out of it like a metal skeleton, but the construction workers hadn't gotten to the point of adding anything like floors or walls yet.

Another flash of white, a glimpse of slick silver hair, caught my eye, whisking up and then dropping behind the body of a crane. My heart thumped faster. My hand came to rest on the gate—right by the lock someone had neglected to fasten.

No one was around. Would it be so horrible for me to slip inside and grab that paper? Even if it didn't turn out to be remotely useful, at least I'd have *tried*.

An eager tingling was already spreading through my chest, deciding the answer for me.

"If I turn up anything interesting, you'll be hearing from me again soon," I said, and hung up the phone before Jemma could ask more questions. I had the feeling if I tried to explain what I was about to do now out loud, it'd sound not just weak but ridiculous.

If Sherlock could shoot himself full of drugs, I could be excused a little risk-taking of my own. At least mine wasn't going to result in bodily or mental harm.

I lifted the latch on the gate and tugged it shut behind me as soon as I was inside. Gravel rattled under my feet. I flicked a fast food wrapper away with my walking stick and headed toward the crane. When my phone jangled with an incoming call, I turned off the ringer.

The wind rose again, making one of the nearby machines creak in a menacing sort of way. The light was continuing to dwindle. I poked all around the crane, squinting, and even peered under it. As I straightened up, the paper I'd come in here after darted past my vision again in the opposite direction. It floated beyond a stack of steel beams.

Fine, then. It wanted to give me a chase, did it? I hurried over, watching in case the breeze flicked it away again.

I didn't see anything move, only felt the faint brush of the air against my cheek, but when I peered around the stack of beams, I'd lost my target again. I let out a huff of breath and scanned the wider area.

There. It must have drifted on over the ground while the beams still hid it. It was trailing along the edge of the pit now, wavering back and forth with shifts in the air currents. I gripped the handle of my walking stick with renewed determination and picked up the chase.

I got close this time—close enough to be sure even in the fading light that it *was* Tillhouse's face in that photograph, close enough to have bent down to snatch at it. The wind picked up at the last instant and whipped the paper from my grasping fingers. It flew right over the edge of the pit and into the thicker shadows below.

I stared after the white shape now skidding down the steep incline. It came to rest on part of the frame just a couple feet from the pit's side. My pulse kicked up another notch as I studied the slope.

For God's sake, I should be able to manage that. I'd tramped all around Iraq, hadn't I? This was nothing. My leg didn't slow me down that much.

I set down my walking stick at the edge of the pit and eased myself over the lip, crouched with my hands pressed against the gritty earth. After a few hesitant footsteps at almost a crabwalk, my confidence grew. I nudged myself onward at a better speed—and that was when it all went wrong.

A loose clod of dirt shifted under my left heel. My foot shot out from under me with a burst of pain through my bad hip. I skidded down the slope too fast to catch myself, the grit scraping my palms raw as I fought to at least keep myself upright.

Despite my efforts, I spun sideways. My thigh and shoulder smacked into the edge of the frame where it loomed close to the pit wall, slamming me to a stop with a fresh sear of agony.

I sat there, panting and staring up at the twenty or so feet I'd fallen, for a long moment. The sharpest shards of pain dulled, but when I adjusted my position to orient myself, my hip ached. It didn't feel as if I'd done it any serious damage, but I might if I tried to scramble back up that slope.

Even if I hadn't hurt myself, I could already tell I'd have a hell of a time making it back to the top. Shit. I couldn't even see the paper I'd been after anymore. It'd disappeared completely.

One of my hands was seeping blood where I'd scraped it. I ran my other hand through my hair, pondering how to get out of this mess. Sherlock wasn't in any real state to help. The thought of calling on Garrett made me wince.

Did I even have cell reception down here? My heart sank as I pulled out my phone. It showed a grand total of one bar, but I knew from experience that might not be strong enough to get me an actual connection. Shit squared.

I gave myself a few minutes to simply breathe and rest my leg. Any excitement I'd been feeling about this expedition had drained away, leaving only a pang of fear. I was about to give the phone a shot just in case when a voice carried down to me.

"John?"

Even distant, I recognized it as Jemma's immediately. "Over here!" I shouted, relief overcoming any embarrassment that welled up at the same time.

Her slim figure appeared at the edge of the pit, the

fading daylight silhouetting her even as it caught on her fiery hair. She cocked her head as she looked down at me, her mouth twisting into a pained grimace. "How did you manage to get yourself down there? *Why* did you go down there?"

"It's a long story," I said, even though it wasn't really, only a ridiculous one. "I hit my bad leg—it's acting up. I'm not sure I can climb out on my own. But you don't want to end up stuck down here too if you—"

"I'll be fine," she said calmly. "And if I'm not, Bash is on his way too. Let's see…"

She picked her way down the steep slope much more gracefully than I'd managed it. With her grasping my arm, I managed to haul myself onto my feet. My hip still ached, but I could ignore that if it meant getting the hell out of this fix.

Jemma had brought my walking stick. She dug the base into the dirt for extra traction as we trudged out of the pit together. Her arm stayed looped around mine, steadying me.

"How did you figure out where I was?" it occurred to me to ask.

"I know at least as many people with many talents as Sherlock does. I had a bad feeling after you hung up. One of my sometime associates tracked your phone. I got rather worried when he reported that the signal had faded out, though."

"I'm lucky I have such a concerned colleague on my side, then."

"Yes, you are." She pulled me up over the edge of the pit and handed my walking stick to me. I grasped it tightly as I regained my balance on the suddenly even ground. Jemma touched my face, and I leaned toward her automatically. The kiss she offered was sweet and soft and over much too quickly.

"I appreciate that you want to explore every avenue to help with our mission," she said quietly, only pulling back a couple inches. "But I would prefer not to lose anyone along the way, all right?"

"I think I can handle that," I said with a brief laugh, but inside my gut had clenched. I wasn't sure I could fully explain how I'd let myself get that far into trouble in the first place. Looking back, the situation seemed absurd.

What had I been thinking? Or rather, why *hadn't* I been thinking? What the hell had come over me?

CHAPTER THIRTEEN

Jemma

Normally if I'd wanted to chat with Garrett—or any of the trio—I'd have picked up my phone. But after the growing uneasiness I'd felt over the last week and John's unexpected stunt last night, I found I wanted to see the detective inspector in person from the start.

There was only so much you could determine from text on a screen or a voice through a speaker. Garrett's part of our mission, on the official law enforcement side of things, was separate enough from what the rest of us were doing that I hadn't seen him face-to-face since we'd started investigating Tillhouse.

So I lingered outside the building across the street from Scotland Yard, partly hidden from the late afternoon sun by an awning, and pretending to be absorbed in the magazine I was holding. The rhythmic rumble of the passing traffic did nothing to set me at ease. Even the sweetness of the sugar cube I'd popped into my mouth only soothed me a little.

He should be finished his shift any minute now. I'd see where he headed off to, and then I'd find a good moment to join him.

My gaze came up without a twitch of my magazine when the door opened. A couple of other officers came out and headed off down the street. A few moments later, Garrett emerged.

I didn't need any detective skills to tell he was upset about something. His jaw was tightly set and his shoulders up, his eyes glowering even though he had no one to glower at right now. He set off around the building toward the parking lot.

If he was driving home, I'd need to catch him before he got in the car. I glanced around to make sure none of his colleagues were within sight and then slipped across the road to catch up with him.

Just as I reached the opposite sidewalk, he paused by a sports car halfway down the lot. His posture turned even tenser, which I wouldn't have thought was possible given how wound up he'd already looked. His hand dug into his pocket, and he drew out something I couldn't see, his gaze fixed on the car. A strange intensity had come over his face.

My pulse skittered. I didn't like that expression at all. I walked as fast as I could without making a scene of it, and his head jerked up at the sound of my footsteps, his hand jamming back into his pocket.

Garrett's eyes widened when he saw me. An even stranger cast came over his features, sickly and stormy at the same time. I didn't know what to make of it, but I could tell it didn't bode well.

"What are you doing here?" he said in a hushed voice.

"I wanted to see you," I said casually, as if dropping in

on him at work were a regular thing. I tipped my head toward the car. "What were you doing? This isn't yours."

Everything else in his face faded under a flush that looked like embarrassment. "No. I—We can't really talk here. Come on. Let's get you away from the Yard."

I kept a professional distance from him as we crossed the rest of the distance to his silver sedan. Garrett motioned for me to get in. He started the engine before I even had my seatbelt on and pulled out of the parking lot swiftly, if not at quite the breakneck pace of John's usual driving.

The inside of the car smelled like Garrett, slightly smoky and electric as a live wire. Usually I enjoyed that scent, but today it made me even more unsettled.

His knuckles had paled where he gripped the wheel. I waited until we'd gotten a few blocks and put his workplace far behind us before I pushed.

"How about you tell me what was going on with that other car now? What did you take out of your pocket?"

"How long were you watching?" Garrett said, his tone unexpectedly sharp. I hadn't heard him sound angry at *me* since we'd all formed our little alliance.

I studied his profile, the flex of his jaw, the continued smolder in his dark brown eyes. "I saw you come out of the building and go into the parking lot. There wasn't much *to* watch. But I could tell you were upset, and I can tell something was going on with that car. Just so you know, the more you try to get around telling me, the more certain I am that I need to find out what it was."

He let out a rough exhalation and swiped a hand through his close-cropped hair. "I just—a few of the other detectives were taking jabs at me this afternoon. Trying to make me look bad to the chief."

I frowned, anger stirring inside me on his behalf. "Assholes. Did you put them in their place?"

"I couldn't really. They weren't saying anything right in front of me, of course. I just caught bits of it, overhearing them when they didn't realize I was close enough… That car belongs to the guy who was making the biggest deal about it. For a second—*just* for a second—I was tempted to jab my pocket knife into one of his tires. Just to slow *him* down a little."

His voice faltered on the last couple sentences, and that shamed flush came back into his cheeks. I blinked at him. "You were seriously considering damaging your colleague's car?"

"Like I said, it was only for a moment."

Even for a moment, that didn't fit with what I knew about Garrett at all. He was competitive, absolutely— sometimes to a fault. But he also had the strictest code of conduct out of the trio. That was why he hadn't been involved in the same activities we had—too much of what even Sherlock and John did in their investigations violated the letter of the law.

The uneasiness that had driven me to seek him out settled heavier in my chest. "Have you been having other moments like that in the last week or so?"

He hesitated just long enough for it to be an answer in itself. "It's just an impulse," he said. "Everyone has them. I ignore them, and it doesn't matter."

"But you've been having them more than usual recently."

"The people I work with have been much bigger arseholes than usual recently!" He caught himself with a grimace. "What are you getting at, Jemma? Are you trying to stay I can't handle this case? Because—"

"*No*," I said quickly. "Why would you even jump to that conclusion? I'm worried about you because I've never seen you act like that. You've been talking differently too… You've all been different."

My hand came to rest on the gold cuff resting against my leg under my dress pants. I hadn't been wearing it constantly like I had when I'd needed to avoid Bog's claim, so it wasn't scraping away at my essence like it had then, but I kept it on whenever I was with any of my men to make sure at least one of us would have a cool head.

Even when I'd taken it off the nights I'd slept alone or when I was working on my own in my apartment, the shrouded folk hadn't hassled me again. Because they'd decided it wasn't worth the bother when I could shut them out again so quickly with the relic?

Or because they'd decided to focus their energies on other targets?

I swallowed hard and took out my phone. "Take us to Sherlock and John's place. I think we need a general strategy meeting."

Garrett's gaze flicked toward me as he took the next right. "Is something wrong?"

"I'd like to say I hope it isn't, but hoping doesn't do much in the face of the facts." I sighed. "We'll see just how wrong it is when we're all together."

"What exactly is the emergency?" Sherlock asked when the five of us were gathered around the now-familiar dining table. His eyes looked brighter than they had the last few days, his movements more animated, but I didn't like the hint of wildness in them, as if some of his perfect control had been worn away. He took a drag from his pipe, the smoke tickling my nose, but the tobacco didn't appear to calm him.

I put a finishing touch on the Fibonacci sequence in the middle of the table—the last of those I'd laid out around the room—and dropped into my seat. I didn't know how well or how long those defenses might last us, but I didn't catch any hint of shrouded folk influence in the air now, so we were at least temporarily safe from their intrusions.

There was no point in beating around the bush. I liked every one of these men because they were straight-shooting. If they couldn't have handled the sort of declaration I was about to make, I wouldn't have been sitting here with them in the first place.

"I think the shrouded folk have determined that the four of you are helping me in my campaign against them," I said, "and they're trying to affect you in malicious ways."

Bash stirred in his chair beside me. "I haven't seen anything."

"Neither have I," Garrett jumped in.

"You wouldn't. They aren't supposed to show themselves. Even the weird lights and figure the one I had the contract with let you see—it's probably been punished for that. But they're allowed to mess with your senses and your minds in ways you wouldn't realize are supernatural."

Sherlock was frowning, and I could already see the denial on Garrett's face, but John was watching me steadily. "What exactly do you think they've done?" he said, in a quiet tone that suggested he could think of at least one example.

I could lead with that incident. I nodded to him. "You saw something yesterday that had you clambering around a construction site and nearly getting yourself stuck down a pit for the night. You could have really injured yourself —you could have even died. But you never did find whatever it was you'd gone after, did you?"

He ignored the concerned and puzzled looks the other shot his way. "No. Are you saying… it wasn't there at all?"

"A shrouded one could easily produce a hallucination. Isn't it odd that you just happened to see something you wanted that badly right when you were passing a spot that dangerous?"

His mouth twisted in a sheepish smile. "You may have a point there. I didn't even think… It never occurred to me."

"I should have warned you. I didn't think they'd go that far." I swept my hair back from my face and turned to Garrett. "And you said you've been hearing things—your colleagues talking behind your back."

Garrett started at me for a moment before he found his voice. "It sounded real enough."

"But you said they've been a lot worse recently. It started after the shrouded folk marked Sherlock, didn't it?"

His posture went rigid. "Yes. But—why would these demons or whatever care about my workplace dynamics?"

I spread my hands. "They just want to mess with you however they can. Make life difficult for you. They obviously decided that was an easy way to provoke you."

The shrouded folk had centuries, maybe even millennia of experience in observing the many negative human emotions. They might be able to read Garrett's weaknesses nearly as well as I could.

"And you," I said to Sherlock. "I don't know if you've seen or heard something, but you've definitely been in an odd mood lately."

John's gaze jerked to his friend. "You have to tell her."

Sherlock stiffened. "I don't see how it's relevant," he said in his usual even tone.

"How *what's* relevant?" I demanded.

"After all these months—it's got to be related," John said. When Sherlock didn't budge, he looked to me. "Fine. *I'll* tell you. He—"

"What John is so concerned about is the fact that I partook of a mild dose of cocaine yesterday," Sherlock interrupted. "It didn't harm me. On the contrary, it alleviated that dour mood you'd observed."

Ah, so that was why I could see a change in him—and why it didn't quite sit right. "Was that really necessary?" I asked.

"It's been ages," John put in. "And you can't be sure— it *was* a problem before."

My eyebrows leapt up. Sherlock's cool demeanor dropped, a look of betrayal crossing his face. "That was a long time ago and is hardly worth mentioning."

"The fact that you won't admit it only shows it's still a potential problem." John's hands clenched on the tabletop. He turned to me again. "When I first moved in, he wasn't as careful with his usage. There were a few times he 'indulged' to the point that he forgot to eat, or he hurt himself accidentally while going around in that state…"

"And I realized more moderation was required and took appropriate steps. I have the situation well in hand, and I have for years. It has nothing to do with these creatures."

I found that just as hard to believe as John clearly did. It didn't seem likely Sherlock would have started using right now after a long dry spell as a total coincidence.

"They haven't gotten to me," Bash said into the silence

that followed. "Maybe these three need to work on their defenses if they're going to stay in the game."

I glanced at him with a pursing of my lips. The way he'd said that told me he wasn't so impervious after all. The shrouded folk were affecting him somehow too— nudging him to be more openly hostile toward the trio.

My stomach had balled into one huge knot. I didn't like this. I didn't like *any* of it. I'd known that bringing the detectives in on my quest would put them in some danger, but I hadn't meant to make their entire lives into a target. I hadn't known the shrouded folk would intrude this far.

"Maybe you should back off," I said abruptly, the words spilling out before I'd totally thought them through. "All of you. I intended to take on these fiends myself, and I can still do that. You had no idea what you were really signing up for when you agreed to help."

The offer to let them loose made my gut tighten even more. We'd made so much progress with all of us working together. Taking down the shrouded folk would be ten times harder without their resources and efforts. But I wasn't going to avenge my sister's death by leading three good men to their deaths as well.

Three, because I already knew there was no way Bash was leaving over this. He grasped my knee under the table. "Forget that. You're not getting rid of me, Majesty."

Perhaps I shouldn't have been surprised, but John leaned his elbows onto the table, his expression just as determined. "You're not getting rid of any of us, Jemma. We're in this now. There's no way we're running off scared."

He'd spoken as if for all of them, and I supposed he could. Garrett was nodding, the set of his mouth defiant.

Sherlock steepled his hands below his chin. "It seems

to me that we're in a much less precarious situation now that we're aware of the possibilities and can be on guard against the creatures' influence," he said. "It also seems to me that your shrouded folk wouldn't be toeing the line of their law so insistently if *they* weren't scared. We're succeeding in pushing them back, aren't we?"

I couldn't deny that logic. "They must be worried about how much we'll accomplish if we keep going. But they could still escalate."

"Then we'll escalate right back," Garrett said, raising his chin. "Face it, Jemma. You roped us in, and now you're stuck with us."

I didn't know whether to laugh or wince at that sentiment. I *had* drawn them in—into what might be the last case of their lives. Even if we rose above everything the shrouded folk threw at us, the fiends clearly weren't going to make the fight easy.

But was this really common sense talking, or was I letting the tenderness I'd started to feel for each of these men sway me into being more afraid of the threat than it warranted? I couldn't let those emotions interfere with choosing the best path, the one that would sever the shrouded folk from this world completely.

I was Jemma Moriarty. I acted from my mind, not my heart.

What would Olivia have thought if she'd known one day I might have let the charms of a few men distract me from the vengeance she deserved?

That final thought hardened my resolve. I stood up and placed my hands on the tabletop.

"All right. We keep going, and we take those bastards down by whatever means necessary."

CHAPTER FOURTEEN

Garrett

The university registrar was being incredibly unhelpful today.

"All I'm asking for is the record from Mr. Tillhouse's admission application," I said, fighting to keep the impatience out of my voice. I spun my pen on my desk, glowering at my computer screen since I couldn't glower at the woman on the other end of the phone line. "It may relate to an ongoing case. I'm assuming there's no government-classified information in your standard application."

"There isn't, but we must keep our standards of privacy, especially regarding our more prominent alumni," the woman said. "If you provide a warrant for the information, we'd could send it to you then."

So much for maintaining helpful relations with the police. "Thank you," I gritted out, and set down the phone with a sigh I couldn't restrain.

"Tough break?" Thompson asked as he passed by my desk.

"Lots of roadblocks. I'll get around them."

I didn't mention how many had already thrown spanners into the works. Tillhouse was a difficult man to investigate. We'd already covered everything on the public record, including his nearly spotless political career, his work as a public defender before that, and a university career apparently free of any major controversy.

The strange thing was, there didn't appear to *be* any public record of Tillhouse's existence prior to his later school days. I'd tracked down a record of him attending a senior school in Sheffield for a couple years, but beyond that the trail went totally cold. It was as if the man hadn't existed until he was thirteen years old. I'd been hoping that his university application might contain more details from his earlier schooling, his family, or something else that we'd find helpful in tackling the MP. Because so far his more recent life had given us nothing to work with.

Thompson walked on, but I heard the tap of his loafers stop just around the corner of the hall. He'd bumped into one of our other constables, because a moment later their hushed voices reached my ears. I went still to pick up the words.

"...at it again," Thompson was murmuring. "As if he can ever prove he deserved to rise that fast."

"I bet it's one of Holmes's whims he's off on anyway," said a voice I recognized as DC Quimble. She made a scoffing sound. "He wouldn't have gotten anywhere otherwise. That's all he does, really—follow the real detective around like a dog."

My shoulders came up instinctively. I dragged in a breath and closed my eyes for a second, jerking my mind back to yesterday evening in Sherlock's flat. To Jemma's obvious concern for us and the suggestions she'd made about the shrouded folk misleading our senses.

Surely Thompson and Quimble wouldn't really carry on like that while I was just around the corner. Thompson had always made a show of friendliness when I was around. Maybe they were talking and some magic was altering their words. Maybe he hadn't even lingered at all and it was a complete hallucination.

I wasn't going to dignify the trick with any acknowledgment. I just had to tune it out and focus on what was important.

I clicked on my track pad, sifting through the files and photographs I'd already accumulated in my file on Tillhouse. Technically I was supposed to be working an extortion case, but I figured saving the world from demonic fiends ought to come first. I'd done some legwork on the other case this morning.

At the desk across from mine, DI Iversley started jiggling his foot. At least, that's what I assumed he was doing. Something, presumably his knee, thumped against the bottom of his desk, making it rattle. That sound was nearly as nerve-wracking as the conversation I was now ignoring.

Someone else in the office was chewing gum incredibly loudly. My fingers twitched as I typed in a search term. Dear Lord, was all of Scotland Yard out to piss me off today? Apparently I should have brought earplugs if I wanted to get anything done.

Of course, the earplugs might not have done a thing if it was all fiendish magic seeping straight into my head.

Maybe it was the chill of that thought throwing me off, or maybe it was simply the culmination of all the irritants that seemed to have battered me at once. One of my colleagues slipped between the cubicles behind me with a muttered, "Bloody minging arsehole," that was clearly directed my way, and I found myself springing to my feet.

"Shut the *fuck* up," I snapped as I spun on the speaker.

The speaker who, from the look on the young constable's face, hadn't said anything at all. Everyone around us stared at me. Including—just my luck—the chief, who I hadn't noticed stepping out of his office.

Bloody hell.

"Lestrade!" he barked. "A word, please?"

I strode over, trying to look nonchalant even though my face was burning. Chief Higgins ushered me into his office. He didn't bother sitting down, just turned to look at me the second he'd closed the door, folding his arms over his chest.

"What the hell has gotten into you, DI?" he said.

"I apologize," I said quickly. "I was overly focused on a case and a little frustrated, and I must have misheard something."

"You should apologize to Kim," Higgins said. "As soon as you go back out there, preferably. And what is this case that's got you so frustrated? From what I saw this morning, everything's on track with that extortion situation."

I hesitated, and his eyes narrowed. "You're handling something else for Holmes, aren't you?"

"You've always said that you appreciate the strong working partnership we've developed," I said.

The chief sighed. "I do—when he's helping you with *our* cases. If he's seen some illegal activity that requires this much of your attention, he needs to bring it to us and get it officially on file. I can't have one of my best investigators going around the office with a storm cloud over his head for any longer. Drop whatever you're doing for him and stick to your assignment. Understood?"

"Yes, sir," I said. Fucking shrouded folk worming their way inside my head. Even knowing they were doing it, I'd let them get to me too much, and now I was in hot water. "I'll get right on that, sir."

"You'd better. I'm going to be keeping a closer eye on you until I'm sure you're back on track. Now get on with it."

I ducked back out of his office, hurried over to the newbie constable to offer a hasty but genuine apology, and then sank into my chair at my desk.

I couldn't hear anyone *talking* about me now, but I was pretty sure I wasn't imagining the fact that many wary glances were being shot my way. I'd made myself look like a fool, shouting like that, and now everyone knew I'd been sanctioned too. Bloody fuck on a fucking bloody cracker.

It was all right. I wasn't losing it. I'd just had a momentary slip. The kind of slip I'd managed to control before it got too bad plenty of times in the past—as recently as yesterday afternoon.

My mind slid back to that violent impulse that had come over me in the parking lot, and to Jemma, afterward, asking what had been going on. She hadn't looked horrified when I'd told her what I'd thought about doing, the way anyone here in the office would have. She'd only showed concern as she tried to figure out what might have been affecting me. It'd been obvious to her that something beyond my normal instincts had been driving me.

It was ridiculous, wasn't it? The person in my life who understood and accepted me most was a criminal mastermind who'd broken God only knew how many laws. But that was the size of it. Even now, my fingers itched to reach for my phone, to reach out to *her*, to reset my balance.

A strange giddy ache spread through my chest. Ridiculous or not, we'd been through a hell of a lot together. I'd tried to keep my distance after the way she'd tricked us when she'd first been in London, but it hadn't worked. She drew me in far too easily. And I wasn't sure anymore that I minded. She might be a criminal, but she had better intentions and loftier goals than most of the police officers I'd met.

What was the point in denying it? I was falling for her. Hook, line, and sinker. I couldn't even blame it on her wiles, not really. I didn't think she *wanted* my adoration. She'd never shown any interest in a real romance.

That was fine. I'd simply feel what I felt and see where it took me. And in the meantime, I was going to find *something* on this bastard Tillhouse for her mission, no matter what the chief had said.

I took a surreptitious glance around to make sure no one could see my computer screen and then went back to the file I'd been sorting through earlier. The only real blank in Tillhouse's life was his childhood. People didn't erase their pasts unless there was something they didn't want discovered, did they? If I just found the right way to dig…

I paused on Tillhouse's year 10 school photograph. His name hadn't gotten me anywhere in my searches. Using our latest facial recognition software, I'd found a few new articles on him that'd been buried in the search results, but I'd offered it recent photographs for that. His adult face had changed a fair bit since his youth. What if I popped this one in?

The facial recognition searches took a while, skimming through the whole internet. I sat back in my chair as the wheel spun, still keeping a close eye on my surroundings, and popped open the paperwork for the extortion case so at least I'd look like I was working on the right thing.

Finally, an alert popped up that the results were ready. I leaned forward to peer at the screen.

The first few were photos I'd already seen from Tillhouse's later school years. Then a slightly grainy shot from a newspaper article came up. I froze in my seat.

It was Tillhouse, all right. The same high forehead and smooth straight hair, the same chiseled chin. He was being clutched to the side of a woman in a group photo with a couple of other families. I'd have guessed he was twelve or thirteen from the looks of him.

Con artists pull off massive bank scam, the article's headline read. A group of grifters had gotten together to arrange to steal a few million dollars from one of the top banks, apparently. They'd nearly managed it, too—and partly with the boy's help. He'd staged a distraction, pretending to be sick, at a key moment.

But one of the guards had realized something was wrong at the last second, and interrupted the grifters before they'd finished their ploy with the accounts. One husband and wife, according to the article, had offered their testimony in exchange for immunity.

The pieces clicked into place in my head. The couple must have been Tillhouse's parents, or he'd have had a juvenile record he couldn't simply have walked away from. No wonder he—maybe the whole family—had changed their name, though. They wouldn't have wanted this attempted crime hanging over their heads.

He'd hidden it awfully deep. It might take some convincing for anyone to believe that the boy in the photo was him after all. But if anyone was good at convincing people, it was Jemma Moriarty.

A smile crossed my lips as I saved the article for future sharing. My colleagues could say whatever they wanted about me, real or imaginary. I got the answers I needed because I was damned dogged about it, not because I'd ridden on anyone's coattails. I'd just proven once more why I'd been the youngest officer promoted to detective inspector in decades.

Now I just had to hope that the lead I'd found would be enough to get rid of Tillhouse and whatever monstrous plans he was an accomplice to now.

CHAPTER FIFTEEN

Jemma

"It was ages ago," Garrett said when I looked up from the article he'd printed out for me. "But it'll set a sort of precedent in the public eye about Tillhouse's behavior —make it more believable if we expose him for something similar."

I rested my arm along the top of my apartment's sofa and raised an eyebrow at Garrett. "But we haven't found anything similar recently to expose him for, have we?"

The embarrassed look that came over his boyish face was rather adorable. "I thought… I don't want to know *how* you do it; I don't want to be involved in that side of things at all… but you did arrange for one man to be arrested and likely sentenced for a crime he didn't commit a few months ago. We can't take Tillhouse down for helping your fiends, so it seems fair to manufacture a real crime to have justice done."

"And to clear our way." I glanced at the grainy photograph on the printout again. The man that boy had become appeared to be interfering with our best efforts to learn more about the Highlands sect of the cult we'd seen some initial signs of. Our additional investigations had produced very little information—not enough to narrow down the location in a helpful way. Records were missing. The local police had balked at helping even Sherlock Holmes. I sensed the influence of a powerful figure there.

And in a year or so, Tillhouse might be the highest authority in this entire country.

I inhaled the crisply clean air of the apartment into my lungs, willing that unnerving thought away. What Garrett had turned up was perfect. As he'd said, it gave us plausibility to make up another crime the MP was connected to. I didn't know if people would open up more if we discredited him, but at least we wouldn't have whatever unknown threat he presented hanging over our heads.

"It's perfect," I said, setting the printout on the coffee table. "And impressive work finding it. More and more I wonder how I ever expected to pull off this mission without your help."

Garrett grinned, but a nervous glint had come into his eyes. There'd been a new awkwardness to his demeanor, subtle but detectable, from the moment he'd come in. Possibly lingering shame over the incident in the parking lot yesterday? He didn't think I thought less of him for that, did he?

"Jemma," he said, "I—"

A knock on the door interrupted him. I held up my hand. "Just a second. That'll be Bash."

Garrett blinked at me as I got up. "I didn't know he was coming."

"Bash is my go-between for all dealings with characters

much more unsavory than me." I winked at him. "If we're going to be doing things you don't want us telling you about, I'm going to need him here to strategize. And it won't be the sort of strategizing we'd want on any phone record."

"Right. Of course."

He didn't look incredibly pleased about Bash's arrival, but I supposed I couldn't blame him when the trio had been faced with the business end of my hitman's gun that once—and also Bash had continued to be testier than usual with the three of them lately. He definitely hadn't escaped the shrouded folk's influence. I'd have bet good money they'd been working on him somehow or other.

That knowledge made my jaw clench on the way to the door, but I managed to relax my expression before I turned the handle. "Come on in," I said to Bash. "We've got lots to do. Garrett brought me a wonderful present."

Bash gave the cop a look that couldn't be interpreted as anything other than skeptical. Garrett had tensed a little on the couch. I suppressed a frown as I returned to take my seat, Bash following me and dropping into one of the armchairs. This alliance we'd formed had worked to my benefit in all sorts of ways, but it could turn catastrophic if too much friction developed between the men around me.

"Sorry," I said to Garrett. "Before Bash and I get down to business, there was something else you wanted to tell me?"

The detective inspector hesitated, his gaze twitching to Bash and back to me. "It was something I only wanted to talk to *you* about. If we could have a moment—or it can wait—"

Bash cleared his throat ominously as Garrett moved to

get up. "Anything you'd say to Jemma you can say in front of me," he said.

I shot him a chiding glance, and he eased back in his chair with just a hint of chagrin. "It's up to you," I said to Garrett. "But I think we should get in the habit of being more open with each other—all of us—unless it's information that would implicate us in a problematic way. And anything along that line that you tell me I'd tell Bash about anyway. You can trust him."

"It's nothing like that." Garrett had stayed on the sofa, but his posture was still tense. He seemed to gather himself, a hint of steel coming into his eyes. "Fine. He might as well hear it too. You've both trusted me enough to let me in on your crazy secret, and— I just want to know that you know who I am."

Bash looked as though he'd restrained an eye roll. I was pretty sure there wasn't anything Garrett could tell me that would shock me, but he was welcome to try. I scooted a little closer and patted his knee. "Go ahead."

Garrett held my gaze. "What happened in the parking lot yesterday—there were times when I was younger that I went through with acts like that. I told you before that I did some rotten things to my older brothers out of jealousy when I was younger, and I didn't mean simple pranks. I sabotaged a school project Mike had spent days working on, I let out one of their pets and because of that it got *killed*, I messed with Carl's shoes before he had a practice and they tripped him up so badly he broke his leg…"

I waited until I was sure he was done. "Is that the worst of it?" I said with a wry but gentle smile.

"It was bad," Garrett insisted, with enough pain in his expression that I knew he felt the remorse all the way down to his bones. "It took seeing one of my brothers in the bloody hospital before I realized how far I'd gone off the rails."

"You were a kid," I said. "In an intense situation where you felt nothing you could do was enough. I remember what you told me. I've *been* in a situation like that. I did far worse than you just said. You've seen what people do to each other in those communes." I swept my hand toward Bash. "And you've met my closest associate. I trust him more than anyone else in the world, and he used to kill people for profit."

He still did, technically, in so much as he was on my payroll, but I suspected it was better not to rub that aspect of our activities in the detective's face.

"It doesn't matter to you," Garret said, not a question. His posture relaxed, and a different sort of light came into his eyes.

"Did you really think it would?"

"I guess—not exactly. I just thought you deserved to know, if we're going to be working together this closely for a while."

I took his hand where it had been resting on the sofa between us. "Garrett, you don't owe me anything. Believe me, I'd let you know if you did."

The corner of his mouth curved upward. "Of course you would. I—I know I should get going so you two can get down to work, but I just—"

He cut himself off and shifted a few inches forward, close enough to tease his fingers along my jaw and tug my mouth to his.

When Garrett kissed, he *really* kissed. The live-wire smell of him filled my nose, and the intensity of his lips sent sparks crackling over my skin. If this was what he needed to trust *himself* to stay the course, I was more than happy to give it to him. I kissed him back eagerly, this good man who must barely be able to conceive of what true evil tasted like.

Bash cleared his throat softly. I ignored him, but Garrett tensed again and started to pull back. I grasped the front of his shirt before he could get very far and turned to look at my hitman.

Bash's expression was rigid. He'd known I got up to all sorts of fun with the trio, but he'd never had to see it.

An idea bubbled up inside me with a giddy energy. I might have the perfect way to undo some of the shrouded folk's influence on my men right here, right now.

I eased my hand up Garrett's lean chest to stroke his neck. "You learned not to be so jealous. How good are you at sharing?"

Understanding dawned on his face. He glanced at Bash with an audible swallow, but his expression looked wary, not disgusted or any of the other more negative reactions I might have gotten.

"Is that what you'd like?" he asked me. "To be shared?"

"I expect I'd like it *very* much. What do you think, Bash? Can you summon a little more of that generous spirit?"

Bash's gaze burned into mine. He paused for long enough that I thought he might refuse.

"It won't be the same without you," I said quietly.

Those words stirred him into action. He got out of the chair and came to me, stopping at the edge of the couch. "Then here I am, Majesty," he said in a low voice. In one swift movement, he leaned in and kissed me, hard.

Mmmm, yes, this was exactly how I liked it. I kissed Bash back with a hand tucked around the back of his neck, and Garrett eased the strap of my silky top to the side to press his lips to my shoulder. Heat kindled all through my body between those points of contact.

Bash kissed me again, his hand traveling down to skim over my breast. At my encouraging murmur, he flicked his thumb firmly over the nipple. Garrett brought his mouth to the crook of my neck and ran his fingers over my thigh. Oh, God, yes. I was caught between the two most possessively intense men I've ever met, and every inch of me was on fire.

When Bash drew back to pull my shirt over my head, I took the opportunity to share another kiss with Garrett. His tongue slipped between my lips as he unhooked my bra. I met it with mine in a hot dueling dance that left us both breathless.

"Still a firecracker," he said hoarsely, caressing my bare breast. "I don't think I'm ever going to get you out of my system, Jemma."

Something twinged, bittersweet, deep in my chest. "I don't want you to," I said with a sudden fierceness, and kissed him again.

Bash had knelt down on the floor by my legs, the perfect position to bring his mouth to my other breast. At the hot swipe of his tongue, I gasped into Garrett's mouth. Pleasure quivered over my skin in every which way.

Garrett's hand slid higher on my leg. I couldn't help arching into his touch when it reached the place between my thighs. Bliss shot through me as he rubbed my clit through my slacks in rhythmic circles. His lips trailed across my cheek and down my neck, and Bash claimed my mouth all over again.

Both of them had far too many clothes on still, but I didn't want to push their comfort levels past the breaking point. Getting naked in front of each other might be a step too far this first time around.

It had *better* only be the first time around. I could already tell I was going to want to repeat this experience.

I slid forward to make it easier for the two of them to remove my slacks, and then we all ended up on the floor, the rug thick and soft beneath us, Bash shoving the coffee table farther to the side. He swiveled his fingers against my panties and growled at the feel of the wetness already forming there. Garrett ground into me from behind, his mouth scorching against my shoulder and his fingers doing wondrous things to my breast.

"Purse," I mumbled, and he grabbed it off the couch in an instant. I reached back to yank down the zipper of his fly. Bash stripped my panties off me as Garrett readied himself.

My breath caught when the head of Garrett's cock pressed between my legs. I eased them a little wider apart, giving him access. He dipped his fingers into my wetness with a groan and then plunged his length into me with a glorious surge of bliss that radiated from my core.

Bash kissed my mouth, and Garrett kissed my neck, the one man fondling my breasts while the other thrust inside me with his hand gripping my hip. Every nerve in my body sang and blazed at the same time. I fumbled with Bash's jeans, my hand shaky with the waves of pleasure rushing through me, and managed to free him from his boxers. His teeth nicked my lip as I gripped his erection.

"Harder," I gasped to Garrett, and he sped up his pace with a ragged curse.

"I want to make you fucking *explode*," he muttered by my ear, his hand teasing around to press against my clit. The determination in his voice combined with the press of his fingers made me do just that. As he bucked into me, my body shuddered and shattered with its release. I gripped Bash harder, pumping him faster. With a clutch of my thigh, Garrett spilled himself inside me.

He stroked his hand over my body, and then he was fishing another packet out of my purse to offer me. "Not only can I share," he said in a voice scorching enough to melt me all over again, "I can take turns too."

Bash let out a chuckle that sounded as if it'd caught him by surprise. I wasn't going to pass up a suggestion that good. I slicked the condom over Bash's length and parted my legs to welcome him.

Garrett kept caressing my side, my breasts, nibbling at my ear and the side of my neck, as Bash thrust inside me. I might have just come, but the rough strokes of my right-hand man's cock filling me sent me soaring all over again. I grasped his bicep and turned my head to kiss Garrett.

"Jemma," Bash gritted out, just my name, as if it were the only word left in his vocabulary. As his pace turned faster, wilder, the friction of his cock sent fresh pleasure searing through me. Turning my head back to him, I started to shudder all over again.

Ecstasy crashed over me. It flooded me and wiped everything else clean. Bash kissed me rough and hard and let out strangled sound as he came.

We lay there on the rug for a few minutes longer, sated and panting—and completely companionable. A smile curled my lips. The shrouded folk could throw whatever they wanted at us, but I'd proven I was stronger. I could win my men back.

Garrett nuzzled my hair and pressed another kiss to my neck. "Jemma," he said, and paused. His voice dropped to a whisper. "I love you."

My pulse hiccupped. I twisted around to face him. "Garrett—"

"I know," he said quickly, his face flushing. "I know that's not what you were looking for. I know that's not what you were offering. I don't expect anything in return. But I wanted to say it, because it's true, and it matters at least as much as the things I told you before."

I sank back into the rug, gazing back at him, but my chest had tightened. Love… that wasn't the sort of seduction I'd ever intended. It wasn't one I had any hope of ever returning. The only person I'd ever really loved had died years ago, and too much of my heart had died with her. After all this time, I wasn't sure even destroying the shrouded folk could heal the wound they'd dealt.

CHAPTER SIXTEEN

Jemma

It was a strange feeling standing surrounded by the four men I knew best in the world with none of them looking like themselves. Of course, I supposed I didn't look much like myself either.

All of us were in full costume for the complex operation we were about to carry out: wigs or temporary dye, plenty of make-up, colored contacts for some, sunglasses for others, new facial hair on all of the guys. Only Sherlock disappeared completely into his disguise with that way he had of transforming even his height and build with shifts in his posture, but I wasn't sure I'd have recognized any of my men at a distance.

I tugged a strand of my sleek blond wig back behind my ear and looked around our circle where we were sitting in the back of a rented van. The space had become humid as soon as we'd turned off the air conditioning, but it wasn't the heat that had my heart thumping faster. We might be all of a half hour from taking down Tillhouse, heading off his sinister plans, and getting a move on with clearing the shrouded folk out of this country.

"Is everyone good to go?" I said. "Any last minute concerns? Let's get them out now, because it's just about time to leave."

"I'm fully prepared and ready to start hollering," Bash said with a flash of a grin. He, John, and Garrett were heading to a political rally Tillhouse was holding here in London, just down the street. Bash had the most prominent job in that part of the operation—he'd be calling out Tillhouse for supposedly siphoning money from his company's investors, hinting that he'd uncovered the politician's criminal history at the same time to provoke a guilty reaction.

Garrett gave me a crooked smile. "My role is pretty simple. I think I can handle placing a single phone call." He was supposedly in attendance as an interested citizen, currently off duty, but he'd call in the disturbance to Scotland Yard to make sure we got a larger police presence on the scene.

"And I'll try to make sure everything stays on track," John said. "Move through the crowd, make a comment here and there to get people talking—easy enough." He rubbed his hands together, clearly eager to jump into the fray.

Sherlock and I were handling the other part of the operation, meant to launch simultaneously with the first for maximum impact. When I glanced at him, his smile looked tight, but it was hard to tell with it partially hidden behind the drooping moustache he'd fixed to his face. "I look forward to playing the supporting character to your leading role," he said in a wry voice that at least didn't sound particularly stressed. His gaze slid to Garrett. "I trust you handled the earlier aspect of your role effectively?"

"They'll be there," the detective inspector said confidently. "I heard them talking about it when I left the office yesterday afternoon." He'd surreptitiously left materials around his office about a special lunch deal for law enforcement at the restaurant where we wanted at least a few of his colleagues to show up.

Every piece accounted for. All those interconnecting elements working in harmony because I had four sharp minds working alongside mine. Sitting there in their midst with exhilaration building inside me, the sense of how much I appreciated these four men hit me like a punch in the gut.

No, not just appreciated. Maybe I couldn't say anything like the three words Garrett had offered me a few days ago, but I cared about them. I would have fought anyone who tried to hurt them. My victory over the shrouded folk would be twice as sweet because it was revenge for preying on them as well as for the many others the fiends had savaged over so many years.

I had the impulse to solidify that bond somehow, to show them how much they'd come to mean to me, but this wasn't the time for it. It wouldn't help to mess up their disguises with a kiss. I settled for grasping John's hand and Garrett's on either side of me and catching Bash's gaze with a tip of my head.

"All right then," I said. "The rally is kicking off now. The three of you get out of here. Knock this asshole out of the picture, and then we can get back to our monster-hunting."

Bash gave me a mock salute. John and Garrett returned my squeeze of their fingers. Then they stood and ducked out of the van, leaving a fizz of worry amid the eager anticipation quivering through my gut.

"Five minutes, and then we set off too?" Sherlock said to confirm.

I nodded, studying him as he leaned back against the van's wall. There was no reason for him to put on much of a false front while we were in here. That sense of gloom still hung over him, didn't it, if milder now? Was it milder because he was successfully battling it or simply because he was taking more care to disguise that too?

"Feeling better now that we've got a clear plan of action?" I asked, keeping my tone light.

"I'd be more pleased if we had any idea what this man's full connection to your shrouded folk is," Sherlock muttered, but he drew himself up straighter a moment later. "I suppose it doesn't matter in comparison to ridding the world of the menace."

"There'll always be plenty of time to question him after we've kicked their shrouded asses to kingdom come."

That remark got me a smile that was small but easier. "I certainly look forward to that moment."

I stood up, smoothed down my posh dress suit, and moved toward the van's door. "Let's get going. We don't want to leave it too long."

We headed down the street in the opposite direction from where the other three had gone. It only took a moment to flag a taxi. The cab wove through the streets to the restaurant where both a group of police officers and some of the employees from one of Tillhouse's more upscale businesses would be taking their lunch. Sherlock sat silently, staring out the window so grimly that I started to worry again.

Before I could prod him a second time, the cab

pulled to a stop at our destination. He sprang out with enough energy to convince me to put the matter to rest until we were done here. As we entered the restaurant, he walked a little behind me, as if he were more my assistant than an equal companion. Always fully immersed in his role.

I spotted Garrett's colleagues with a quick scan of the elegant interior. The officers looked as though they felt a tad out of place among the white table clothes and gleaming silver fixtures, but they were chatting away between bites of their lunches and glances at their surroundings. Our primary target, the company's CFO, was eating on his own meal with a tablet propped on the table beside him, either reading or still working while he finished his food.

The maître d hustled over. "A table for two?"

"We don't need a new one," I said in a haughty tone. "I see the person we're here to meet right over there."

I set off toward the CFO with brisk strides and my head held high. I needed to look believably like the sort of woman who might have invested a large sum in stocks for an international merchandising corporation. My footsteps and Sherlock's behind me thumped dully on the dense carpet.

The maître d had trailed after us as if to make sure we really were expected. I hoped he wouldn't cause too much trouble, but if he did, Sherlock would take care of that for long enough for me to get my piece in.

We were just one table away when the detective grabbed my elbow. I hesitated as he pulled closer to me.

"We can't use him," he murmured by my ear in an urgent voice.

I stared at him. We'd chosen the man by group

consensus two nights ago. "Why not?" I asked under my breath.

Sherlock grimaced. "He's got a splotch of mud on his trousers. It's a distinctive color—one I've seen on Tillhouse's before. One I determined is specific to a country club near here. No doubt they both belong to it. There wasn't any evidence of that before. Now I'd be inclined to believe the two are friends more than distant business associates."

From anyone else, that reasoning would have sounded like a stretch. From Sherlock, I had to assume he was putting together several other minute pieces he didn't have time to get into. He wouldn't have stopped me in the middle of our operation if he hadn't thought there was a real chance we'd gotten off course.

If the CFO had a personal loyalty to Tillhouse, confronting him might not have the effect we wanted. We needed someone who'd focus more on getting to the bottom of the problem than ensuring peace of mind for the man behind the scenes.

My heart stuttering, I cast my gaze about as the maître d cleared his throat behind us. Thankfully we hadn't gotten quite close enough to the CFO for it to be obvious we were now changing our minds. Several employees from the company, which had its offices just down the street, tended to lunch here. The CFO was only the most prominent. We could just as easily use…

My gaze settled on a man I recognized from the company records we'd gotten our hands on. A couple of steps down the ladder from the CFO here, but on the accounts side of things, which worked just fine. I even remembered his name, because it fit his appearance so well: Marten. He looked like a marten, ruddy haired and weaselly.

I shifted direction with an air as if I'd taken a slight detour on purpose and marched up to Mr. Marten's table. He was sitting with a woman I didn't recognize, at least ten years younger and her clothes clearly off-the-rack rather than tailored like most of the senior employees. One of the secretaries, I'd bet. I'd put a fair amount of money on the possibility that Marten was sleeping with her too, although that had little bearing on our success here.

"Mr. Marten," I said in a sharp voice pitched to carry through the room. "I'm very concerned about the state of my accounts. The math does *not* appear to be adding up."

Marten blinked at me, his jaw freezing in mid-bite, but I'd spoken with enough authority that he had to assume he knew me even if he hadn't the slightest clue who I was.

"I'm sorry, madam," he said, fumbling. "I'm not sure what you mean?"

"My shares in Everring Marketing." I whipped out my phone open to the account—an account my and Sherlock's associates had conjured up in preparation for this confrontation. "Look at these numbers. With the percentage rise in the stock yesterday, I should have seen an increase of *twice* that much. It concerned me so much I looked back through my past statements and found *repeated* omissions across *years*. I need answers, now!"

"Ma'am," the maître d said with a wringing of his hands, and Sherlock intercepted him smoothly with some murmured distraction. From the corner of my eye, I saw the cops glancing our way.

Marten took the phone from me and peered at it. His

eyes widened for a second before he caught his expression, but he clearly saw the discrepancy too. "I—I'm not sure what's going on here," he said. "If you could come into the office—"

"Into the office?" I cried. "What, so you can rob me even more? This is a disgrace. Tens of thousands of dollars taken from under my nose, and you don't know what's 'going on'?"

"Really, at this point we should call the police," Sherlock said in a high, stilted voice. "How can we trust people who've been robbing you for nearly a decade?"

As intended, a couple of the officers from the nearby table got up and strolled over. "What seems to be the problem?" the woman in the lead asked.

Marten blustered something about taking care of things internally, and the CFO slunk over to see what was going on, but I let the officers usher me off to the side where neither of the company's employees had to be part of the conversation. With much dramatics, I explained the supposedly missing money. "I wouldn't be surprised if it's all sorts of people," I finished off with. "Ripping off their stockholders left and right. It needs a full investigation."

As the woman reassured me that someone would look into it, the man with her got a call. He turned away from us to answer it and swiveled back a few moments later with a bemused expression.

"You'll never believe it," he murmured to the woman. "There's been another incident about this just now."

"Stay here in case we have any more questions, please," the woman said to me, and went off with the man to get the details. I exchanged a triumphant glance with Sherlock. At the same moment, my own phone buzzed.

It was a text from John. *All went well. Your man put on*

quite the show. Everyone's talking now. Couldn't have asked for a better blow-up.

A smile curled my lips as I sent him a thumbs up in response to indicate our own part of the plan had gone off successfully despite its momentary hitch. A sense of satisfaction settled over me, tinged with not a little relief.

One major obstacle removed; one potentially horrific threat demobilized for long enough that we should be able to clear out his supernatural support and end whatever the shrouded folk had intended to accomplish here. We'd won the battle—now it was time to win the war.

Sherlock

I jerked awake with a wrenching sensation around my limbs. In the dark room, I yanked against my apparent bindings instinctively. It took my exhausted brain a few seconds to register that I wasn't tied up by anything other than my twisted sheet.

I sank back into the mattress. The air conditioner whirred, turning my skin clammy with the sweat that had broken out over it in my sleep. In my sleep, and in the middle of whatever dark, ominous dream had sent me jolting out of slumber in a panic for the fifth time since I'd taken to bed last night.

The contents of those dreams eluded me. I had no idea what in them had been so terrifying. All I was left with when I woke up was the racing of my heart and the cold sweat on my skin—and the distinct impression that something essential was slipping from my grasp far too quickly.

It wasn't a sensation I enjoyed. I breathed slowly and

deeply, taking my mind through the paces of a few simple meditation exercises, but my nervous system remained on high alert.

I *should* have had better control over myself. I normally did.

No doubt it didn't help matters that my sleep had been so broken. I might have gotten four hours of truly restful sleep, if that much, across the past nine of trying. Each time I'd woken up in this state it'd taken me a long time to settle myself enough to drift off again.

I stared up at my plaster ceiling, tracing the familiar paths with my gaze. My eyelids felt heavy and my head muggy, but my heart thumped on and my thoughts were whirling. Morning sunlight was seeping insistently past my curtain. I wasn't sure there was any point in trying to add to my rest for the day. If I wasn't up soon, John would become concerned, and that would only add another layer to my difficulties.

I'd functioned on less sleep before. I could manage one day like this.

And I wouldn't think about the possible causes of my nighttime disturbances. It wasn't as if I could tackle them directly as it was.

There were other things I could tackle if I got out of this bed. I shoved back the covers and methodically changed into suitable clothes for the day. Then I reached for my phone and texted Garrett.

Any additional word on the proceedings regarding Tillhouse?

I set the phone down, not expecting an immediate answer, but it rang a second later with an incoming call. Apparently Garrett had gotten into the office early—or he was monitoring proceedings from afar.

"You're not going to like this," he said grimly when I picked up. "The bastards are releasing him. He's convinced them that it's impossible he 'engaged in any wrongdoing'."

My stomach plummeted. No. It didn't make sense. It shouldn't have been possible. We'd set up everything within the accounts to make an airtight case.

"How could he possibly have done that?" I demanded.

Garrett let out a huff of breath that expressed nearly as much frustration as was coursing through me. "I haven't got a bloody clue. I can't get a straight answer—no one's keen to talk about it. But after everything we've seen... I wouldn't be surprised if Jemma's shrouded folk had a hand in it."

That possibility brought a sour taste into my mouth. Yes, why wouldn't Jemma's creatures be involved in influencing events around this case if the man was tied up in their schemes? He had to be awfully important for them to have taken a gamble on someone outside their cult.

But if that were the case... was he simply untouchable?

"There *has* to be a way we can make something stick," I said, the words coming out more vehemently than they might have if I'd been properly alert.

"Maybe Jemma will have some ideas. I'll keep prodding the detectives involved about how exactly he turned the tables. Or possibly we'll be able to circumvent him completely, if he's going to be this much of a pain in the arse."

We both knew we couldn't simply ignore Tillhouse, though. He represented the largest violation these monsters had made within our world—their most blatant grab for power. Damn it.

"I just got off the phone with someone at the station,"

Garrett said. "I was going to check in with Jemma, and we'll go from there. I expect you'll hear from me again before much longer."

"Yes, keep me apprised of the situation."

I tossed the phone onto my bed, walked toward the bedroom door, halted, and walked back again. Where the hell was I going? Where the hell *could* I go? For fuck's sake, the blasted shrouded folk could be in this room right now and I'd never know it. They left no traces, no clues I could easily decipher.

I came to a stop by the dresser with one of Jemma's mathematical sequences laid out across it. She'd brought decorative stones to give her patterns a more appealing look, as if I cared much about whether the things were easy on the eyes as long as they worked.

They didn't, clearly, if the creatures were sabotaging my very sleep.

The clink of dishes sounded from the other side of the door. John was moving about the common room now, making his breakfast no doubt. I couldn't summon a spot of hunger myself. And as I listened, he started humming —a slightly off-key but buoyant tune that would have made me smile fondly most other days. Today, my gut clenched in resistance.

I wasn't going to be good company for him in my current state of mind. His optimism would only irritate me, and I wasn't certain I had the capacity to completely hold my temper. Better I kept to myself as I normally did when I had a problem to work through.

A thought passed through my head as clear as my own voice. *So you finally met a case you can't crack, Sherlock.*

"I'll crack it," I said under my breath. "I just need more time."

How much time have you had already? They've gotten the better of you—there's no other way of looking at it.

It wasn't unusual for me to talk to myself while I was working my way out of a problem, but my sparring partner in those internal conversations wasn't normally so hostile. My frustrations had obviously seeped all through my consciousness.

"I'm not beaten."

Oh, no? You look an awful lot like you are. What exactly are you accomplishing right now?

My teeth gritted. "There has to be something I've missed. I *will* find it. Every crime leaves a trail behind—supernatural ones can't be any different." I refused to allow them to be.

I jerked open my work drawer on my dresser and grabbed the various printouts, clippings, and reports I'd gathered over the course of the case. The folders felt far too light in my hands. I fished out paper after paper and laid them all out across the bed, pausing just for a moment to jerk straight the covers.

There were enough pieces that they had to overlap. I squinted at them, rearranging them into clearer patterns, scowling at them when nothing new immediately emerged.

Patience. I could have patience. One at a time, read them over, study every picture. There would be a clue in there. I only had to piece it together.

Reading took longer than usual. My fatigued mind tripped over the words here and there. I rubbed my eyes and tried to focus more intently.

When my phone chimed with an incoming text, I ignored it. Whoever wanted me, they could wait. Nothing was more important than this.

By the time I'd made it through the spread of papers at one corner of the bed, an ache was building behind my eyes.

John rapped his knuckles on my door. "Sherlock? Are you up?"

"I am. Just going over some notes."

He paused. "Garrett said he told you the news. I can't believe they're ready to let Tillhouse off without even a full investigation."

"It is a rather ridiculous turn of events," I agreed. His voice made my headache pulse harder.

"I don't know if you saw—we're going to meet up to discuss next steps. I could tell everyone to head over here—"

"No," I said, quickly and emphatically. "I'm going to bow this one out, and I can't have any disruptions. I'm— I'm close to the answer. I can feel it. Arrange your meeting elsewhere and make whatever plans you can. I won't have anything constructive to contribute until I work my way through this."

John didn't disguise the concern in his voice. "Are you sure? Your insight is always going to be valuable—"

"I'd like that period without disruptions to start now."

"Ah. All right then. I'll leave you to it. If you need any of us, you know how to reach us."

I'd expected to feel relief at his leaving. I stood stock still until I heard the thump of the outer door shutting and the click of his key turning the lock. Then I turned back to my spread of papers—the *mess* of papers, really, because it couldn't be called anything like orderly at this point—and a wave of utter hopelessness rolled over me. It pressed down on me like a boulder, heavier than I'd ever felt this sort of uncertainty before.

It wasn't the same sort of uncertainty at all, was it? Before I'd only been dealing with the habits of human beings, predictable as long as you could ferret out all the facts. Now I was dealing with the completely unknowable.

I'd pulled back the curtain to let in the sunlight, but in that moment the whole room wavered darker. The gloom had descended on me so thickly it was shadowing my vision. I was drowning in it, in dark water closing over my head. My lungs constricted as I dragged air into them.

Who was I, if I didn't have a mind sharp enough to penetrate this problem? What use was I at all—what point was there to all the studies I'd done and the exercises with which I'd honed my senses, if I couldn't stand up to the first truly expansive threat I'd ever faced?

For an instant, my throat closed up completely. Doubt suffocated me. A chill of fear prickled after it, penetrating right down to my center.

I wasn't going to think through anything when the depression settled over me this heavily. That was what the creatures would want, wasn't it—to see me incapacitated by my frustration? But I had tools they couldn't have anticipated. I could shock myself out of this state.

I *had* to.

John was long gone, but I still glanced around the common room when I came out, noting the absence of his walking stick, which he normally left by the umbrella stand next to the door, and his favorite hat gone as well. Wherever they'd ended up arranging their meeting, he shouldn't be back for some time. I could jumpstart my mental faculties in a matter of minutes and get down to work as I was meant to be doing.

I took a freshly washed glass from the dishwasher and brought it back to my room. Then I retrieved the locked box from my closet, along with a jug of distilled water. With careful precision, I poured some of the water into the glass and took the baggie of white powder and a measuring spoon from the box.

One of these spoonfuls was the dosage I'd decided on. I'd already taken it twice in the last week, and it'd only partly and briefly stirred me out of my dark state. I glanced at the scattered papers on the bed, and resolve gripped me.

I'd set that limit in consideration of the way I'd abused the substance in the past. It had been decided out of extreme caution, nowhere near any level that should be considered dangerous. What was bloody well dangerous was letting those monsters and the man they were backing roam free while I wandered in this hapless daze.

I dropped one spoonful into the glass and dug the instrument into the powder again. If there was going to be any point in taking this route, I needed to set caution aside and go all in.

Anything it took to break me free of this rut and win the day after all would be worth it.

CHAPTER EIGHTEEN

Jemma

Bash set a hand on my arm, and I looked up from my laptop's screen. Beyond the windshield of the car we were staked out in, an elderly woman was picking her way rather nimbly across her front yard between the rock garden and the ash tree. She didn't glance our way. Really, there was no reason for her to be suspicious of an old station wagon parked one house down on the other side of the street. I went back to my work.

"Do you think she knows?" Bash asked.

The woman was Tillhouse's mother. His parents had been living in this house since shortly after they'd all changed their names and gotten the heck out of dodge some forty years ago.

"About the details?" I said. "Hard to say. But even if they don't, there could still be *something* telling in here."

With advice from one of my particularly computer savvy contacts, I'd hacked into the house's home network and from there gotten access to the email accounts of the senior Tillhouses. Thank the Lord they were technologically inclined, or we'd have had to resort to digging through their literal trash.

Instead, I'd skimmed back through several years of saved emails and was now checking the spam folders.

Bash's phone dinged with a text. He glanced at it. "John says they've finished their visit to the local police station."

"Tell them to go back to that diner where we got lunch, and we'll meet them there in a half hour or so. I'm almost finished here." So far I hadn't turned up anything that looked all that useful, although I'd copied all the emails between the MP and his parents over to my hard drive for further perusing later.

There had to be something *somewhere* that could knock Tillhouse down—or at least remove him from the picture for long enough that we could make a real move on the commune that must be most directly supporting him. Our further investigations over the last couple weeks hadn't turned up any clearer patterns of activity in the country other than the ones we'd already identified. We'd taken down one sect, and another had fled. That only left our enemies in the Highlands to deal with.

Too bad there were a hell of a lot of Highlands, and apparently not all that many people in Scotland who were willing to lend us a hand.

Children laughed where they were playing somewhere down the street. I sank deeper into my seat, propping the laptop's screen against the wheel. Amazing how many junk mail messages you could manage to get in a month. None of them had anything constructive to offer, though.

My last place to consider was the digital trash. In there, I found more spam that hadn't been properly filtered and not a whole lot else. Tillhouse's parents didn't get a whole lot of expected electronic communications. I'd sucked my lower lip under my teeth, my gaze slipping down over the list of subject lines, when I stopped with a jolt of excitement.

A perfect deal for another fantastic Scottish vacation!

Bash shifted in his seat as I clicked the email open, alert to my change in mood. "Did you find something?"

"Maybe." I scanned the email's contents, and a small smile curled my lips. "Yes. It's not definitive, but— apparently the parents had a little Scottish vacation sometime last year. A country resort 'nestled in the Highlands.' It could be totally unrelated, but from what I've seen, their son pays for any luxuries they have. If he was buying them a vacation, he'd probably pick an area he's familiar with. They might even have their own part to play with the commune."

"Does it fit with the patterns of behavior the Londoners found before?"

I switched to the map and checked the resort's location. "It's within the broad area we were looking at. That could narrow things down quite a bit. At the very least, we can make a more focused effort around those parts now."

I flicked through the rest of the trash folder just in case, not really expecting another prize. Then I closed the laptop, tossed it in the back, and started the engine. "Let's see what our detectives scrounged up."

John's car was already parked in the lot of the diner where we'd eaten. A trace of berry sweetness from the tart I'd finished my lunch off with still lingered in my mouth. Maybe I'd grab another of those while we talked.

This road trip had been a rather impromptu one. We'd

been discussing Tillhouse's release in frustration, and Garrett had made a comment about delving into the guy's history directly, and somehow we'd all ended up deciding to come up here and check out the area where he'd spent his later formative years.

Well, all of us except for Sherlock, who was apparently absorbed in some brainstorm he hadn't bothered to give even John any details about. I'd been tempted to nudge the consulting detective with a text and find out where his thoughts were headed, but John had forbidden any contact.

"When he gets in that state, he'll take your head off for interrupting him," he'd said. "He'll get to whatever inspiration he's chasing down faster if we leave him to it."

Now, Bash and I found Garrett and John sitting in the exact same booth, already near the bottom of their mugs of coffee and John halfway through a slice of the lemon cheesecake I'd been eyeing on the menu along with the tarts.

I plopped down across from them and promptly stole a bite of the cheesecake. John gave me an amused look as my eyes rolled upward in ecstatic appreciation. I flagged down the waitress to order a slice all for myself and then set my elbows on the table to get down to business.

"Our man's parents went on a trip to the Highlands not too long ago," I announced. "Interesting choice, don't you think?"

John perked up. "Do you figure they'd have been near the commune up there?"

I shared the same reasoning with them I'd offered Bash. My cheesecake arrived, and after I'd taken my first bite, I waved my fork in the direction of the detectives. "Did you two turn anything up?"

Garrett shook his head. "No patterns of crime or connections to Scotland that we could find—which really, we should have expected. Tillhouse wouldn't have wanted to let the criminal side of his dealings connect too closely to his home ground."

"It was worth checking, though," John said. "And obviously it's a good thing we came up here, given what Jemma found. So, what's next? We pay this vacation spot a visit and see what the word is around there?" His eyes shone with the excitement of having a mission ahead.

"If we're going to make our own trip to Scotland, I think our first stop should be the police," Garrett said. "It'll be harder for them to turn me away in person."

Bash let out a scoffing sound. "They wouldn't help you at all before—why would they change their tune now? They'll probably give you a load of bull that points us in the wrong direction just to get you off their backs."

Garrett glowered at him. The intimacy the three of us had shared a few days ago might have broken down a few hostilities, but it was hard to say the two of them had exactly become friends. Their personalities clashed too much.

"I didn't get to the position I'm in by giving up too easily," the detective inspector said. "And whatever your opinions on the police force are, we *do* tend to be loyal to each other with the right motivation."

"I think we should start with Jemma's lead," John jumped in. "It's the most concrete one we have. Then we might have more details to direct the questions we want to ask the police."

Garrett frowned. "If we start nosing around a place where Tillhouse has connections, that could tip him off that we're getting close, especially since he's probably even more on guard after the blow-up yesterday."

"How many people can he even have alerted at this point?" Bash protested. "He just got released from custody this morning, and they're off in some remote spot away from civilization. It's not like it'd take a simple phone call."

"We don't know that for sure."

"Whoa, whoa," I said, holding up my hands. The debate was setting my nerves on edge. It sounded like too much petty squabbling and not like a team working together. Possibly because we didn't have the whole team together.

But it wasn't just that, was it? Even now, even after the shrouded folk had cast a shadow over these men in various ways, the threat wasn't real to them the way it was to me. They might have seen photographs and witnessed injuries and heard my reports, but I'd seen one of those screaming violent deaths with my own eyes. I'd lived amid that violence for fourteen years.

My gut knotted. Taking down this commune, wiping out the others until the shrouded folk could no longer maintain their presence here in our realm—it wasn't just another, albeit particularly immense, case. It was a matter of human survival. There was too much at stake here to be sniping at each other over strategy.

This really was a war, and even now, none of the men around me could fully comprehend that.

"We're not doing *anything* today," I went on. "Garrett, Scotland Yard expects you back there tomorrow, don't they? And maybe we can still salvage our campaign against Tillhouse somehow once more information comes out. We need to find out what Sherlock's been up to all this time.

We'll regroup, all five of us, pool our resources, and make a proper plan of attack for heading north."

Garrett winced. "Sorry," he said. "It's just so maddening that he's walking free—I got carried away."

"And we really should loop Sherlock back in," John said with a sheepish expression. "He may have wrapped this whole thing up while we've been running around."

I perked up as I popped another bite of lemon cheesecake into my mouth. "Have you heard from him?"

He shook his head. "I'll give him a nudge in warning when I'm almost back at the flat. Maybe we can have that meeting there over dinner." He glanced at the clock on the diner's back wall. "And I guess we should head out if we want to be back in London in *time* for dinner."

I jabbed at my cake. "Let me finish this, and we'll get going."

Evening was starting to settle in when Bash and I reached central London. We'd switched places in the car, him driving and me poring over Tillhouse's emails with his parents, but I hadn't turned up any clues. All I'd gotten was an ache behind my eyes. I rubbed them and closed the laptop, and my phone vibrated with an incoming call.

It was John. "Are we on for dinner?" I asked him.

"I don't know," he said with worry laced through his voice. "We're about ten minutes from Baker Street now. I texted Sherlock five minutes ago, and just called, and he's not answering."

A thread of cold wound through me from throat to stomach. "Is that unusual when he's absorbed in work?" I asked.

"I don't think he'd ignore his phone completely, especially when he knows we've been out doing our own work. For all he knows, he's missing news about Tillhouse or some other aspect of the case."

"Maybe his battery died."

"It could be. He's normally pretty fastidious about that."

My fingers tightened around my phone. "So, what are you thinking?"

"I don't know." John sighed. "It's probably nothing. He left the phone in the other room and got so caught up in thought he didn't hear it, something like that. I just don't like it."

"We'll come," I said firmly. "If he doesn't want a dinner meeting, he should have picked up the phone to tell you so." I'd rather meet an irritated Sherlock than sit with this anxiety twisted all through me.

He hadn't seemed completely like himself for a while now. The shrouded folk had been acting on him in ways he hadn't wanted to admit. They wouldn't have outright *attacked* him, would they? The possibility seemed incredibly unlikely given what I knew about them, but it also made me queasy.

"Drive faster," I told Bash. "Let's get to Baker Street."

He took the next few turns at just shy of dangerous speed, only slowing at a glimpse of a police car. We made it to Sherlock and John's building just as John and Garrett were pulling up outside.

John hustled up the stairs to the apartment with his mouth set in a tense line. "Sherlock?" he said as he unlocked the door and pushed it open. "We gave you as long as we could manage without any disruptions. I'm afraid you're going to have to put up with one now."

We got no answer. The living room was empty, the dining table bare, no sign of recent activity out here. Sherlock's bedroom door was closed.

John's posture had stiffened. He set his walking stick aside so abruptly it fell over with a clatter, but he didn't stop to pick it up. He strode to Sherlock's door with his slightly uneven gait and knocked. "Sherlock? Sherlock!"

The knob didn't budge when he rattled it. "Could he have gone out?" I said. "He might not even be here."

John's hand dropped from the door knob. "You're right. He could—" He froze, his eyes widening, and took a long inhale.

"I smell vomit," he said in a thin voice, and dashed across the apartment to his own room heedless of the wobble that speed brought into his leg. I'd already reached Sherlock's bedroom when John emerged a second later, unwrapping a set of lock picks. A faint whiff of that sour scent reached my nose, and my stomach turned.

"For the first time, I'm glad he insisted on badgering me into learning how to use these," John muttered, but his voice was taut with distress. His hands shook as he wielded the picks.

"Let me," I said.

He handed them over without protest. I inserted them into the keyhole and flipped the lock in a couple of seconds with a frantic jerk of my hands. The instant I'd pulled the picks out, John was shoving the door open.

A choked sound escaped his throat. Sherlock was sprawled on his side on the floor, his face blotchy, vomit streaking the hardwood by his mouth. John dropped at his side, grabbing his hand to check for a pulse. As I dashed after him, my pulse rattling through my veins, my gaze fell on the box lying open on the bedspread. On the baggy of white powder, nearly empty, and a syringe with a bead of liquid still poised at the tip of its needle.

This was war, all right. And the shrouded folk had found the perfect weapon to land a killing blow.

A nearly killing blow. "He's alive!" John said. "Barely. Someone call an ambulance!"

"Already have," Garrett said from the door, looking shocked.

I knelt down beside John, steeling myself against the hopeless sensation that rose up at seeing Sherlock so frail. "Tell me what we have to do to make sure he stays with us."

CHAPTER NINETEEN

Jemma

The hospital had exactly the sort of aesthetic I should have enjoyed: straight lines and clean whites and beiges. Something in the atmosphere cast too much of a shadow over it, though—the undertone of heavy disinfectant, the beeping of machines measuring the strength of lives in peril. Or perhaps just the knowledge that one of those lives belonged to the only man I'd ever felt could match me on every front.

At first, we'd all ended up in the waiting room while the doctors did what they could for Sherlock. Bash had stayed mainly to support me, and when it'd become obvious he felt awkward lingering there, I'd sent him back to his apartment. Garrett had left a little while after that, saying the best thing he could do for the man was get to the bottom of Tillhouse's release.

That left John and me. The former surgeon had alternately sprawled on the stiff waiting room chairs and paced across the linoleum floor with sharp jerks of his walking stick, his gaze nearly always fixed on the hallway that led to the treatment rooms.

They hadn't let us see Sherlock yet, hadn't told us anything other than they were giving him the best possible care, however reassuring that was supposed to be.

I'd come across overdoses before—among junkies and other unstable characters. Even after John had mentioned Sherlock was using again after a stretch of sobriety, I'd never thought I'd find myself here waiting to find out if the world's foremost detective had survived his own over-indulgence.

How much had his own innate moods gotten the better of him in this frustrating and unnerving situation, and how much had the shrouded folk given him a direct push? Even he might not be able to tell us accurately. I knew how slyly the fiends could exert their will.

I popped a sugar cube into my mouth, my fourth of the evening, although the sweetness only cut a tiny bit of the worry souring my stomach. John marched over to the nurse's desk again.

"Is there any news at all?" he said. "Is he in recovery? When will we be able to see him?"

"I haven't gotten any updates," the nurse said in a mild but weary voice. "I'll be sure to let you know as soon as I do. From what I've seen, with cases like that, it might be a while yet. If you're going to stay, you should settle in for a long wait."

John let out his breath in a rough exhalation and meandered back toward me. The normally cheerful light in his hazel eyes had dulled to a faint, frantic glimmer. Where his appearance normally gave the impression of warmth and softness, the muscles in his broad shoulders and along his jaw had turned hard with tension. It made my own gut knot tighter seeing him like that.

I got up just before he reached me and grasped his wrist. "Why don't we find the cafeteria and get something to eat while it's still open? You're only going to feel worse if you starve yourself."

John's posture stiffened even more. "If something comes up about Sherlock—"

"We won't be gone that long. Anyway, I heard what she told you. It could be hours more before we get any real news."

He grimaced, but his stance relaxed a little, enough that I could tug him along with me.

"I'm not sure I can stomach much right now," he remarked.

Neither was I. "Well, we'll try our best," I said, attempting to insert his usual cheer into the vacuum left by his distress.

We headed down the hall toward the staircase that led to the lower level. John kept twitching his walking stick restlessly. If anything, now that we'd left the waiting room he looked even more pained than he had before.

"You know it isn't your fault, don't you?" I said.

"How can *you* know that? I live with him. I'm his best friend—practically his only real friend. I knew he was using again. I should have realized something was wrong when he put me off this morning—I should have insisted on staying…"

He trailed off as if realizing even in his furor how ridiculous that idea was. I gave him a gentle teasing nudge. "And, what, you would have sat in the living room while he worked away in his bedroom, and still not have known what he was getting up to? Do you really think he'd have agreed to hourly check-ins or anything else like that? He'd probably have come up with some quest of his own to send you on if he'd wanted privacy that badly."

"Yes." John sighed and rubbed his hand over his face. "But still. My whole job is to support him, to fill in the gaps when he can't handle everything on his own. If I can't even make sure he stays *alive*, what the hell good am I?"

Those words sent a jab through my chest. I grasped John's wrist again and turned him toward me so I could look him right in the eyes.

"He's a grown man. It was his job to look after himself. He could have told any of us if he was struggling more than he let on. And you are *not* Sherlock's keeper. You're more than just his goddamned sidekick. How many people did you save before you even met him? I don't care how brilliant or lauded a detective he is—it doesn't mean you stop mattering."

John blinked at me, clearly startled. Then he closed his eyes. "I know that," he said quietly. "I know all of that, but it still kills me that I couldn't stop this somehow, that I can't do anything now."

I drew him into an embrace, tucking my head against his shoulder. An orderly trotted by us without a second glance—no doubt people hugging out their fears or grief was a pretty common sight in the hospital halls.

John let out a shaky breath and wrapped his arms around me, pulling me closer. For a few minutes, we just stood there, locked together in the little comfort we could manage to generate between us.

When John eased back, he kept his head bowed over

me, his forehead nearly grazing mine. He held my gaze for a long moment.

"It bothers you almost as much as it bothers me, doesn't it?" he said. If he sounded a little startled by that too, I suppose I deserved that.

I started to speak and found a lump had risen in my throat. "He's a spectacular man. I hadn't known there was anyone like him in the world. Now it seems like a pretty horrible thing that the world might lose him."

The corner of John's mouth quirked up just slightly. "So it's the world's loss you're concerned about, not your own?"

"It's all the same thing, really." An ache spread from my throat down through my chest. "But just so you know, the thought of losing you or Garrett upsets me just as much. If you start to feel you've been pushed to close to some edge—"

"I know." He touched my cheek. "I swear I'll tell you if anything's wrong. You don't need to worry about that."

The tingle of his breath across my face woke up other feelings far less fraught than my fears. A quiver traveled down through my core. There were other sorts of comfort, other avenues for release when there was no fully escaping the horrible situation you'd found yourself in. I suspected John could use the distraction as much as I did, if not more.

"Show me," I murmured, resting my hand on his chest. "Prove to me how much you're here with me."

The thump of his heart beneath my palm sped up. John hesitated, his gaze flicking to one side and then the other to confirm we were alone in the hall, and then he ducked his head to capture my mouth.

There was an urgency to his kiss I'd never felt from him before—he was usually so gentle even at his most passionate. The hunger that had stirred in me before woke up completely, as if I were famished for this. I kissed him back just as hard, my fingers gripping the front of his shirt, my head tilting to allow him better access to my mouth.

John made a rough sound and shoved me half a foot back so my shoulders jarred against the wall. The impact only heightened the thrill. Our tongues dueled, and his heat soaked right through me. It might not have been able to wash away all the anxieties of the day, but it could overwhelm them while we were in the middle of this collision.

I tore my lips from his just long enough to gulp air and spot the door to a closet some ten feet down the hall. My hand still fisted in John's shirt, I yanked him with me, threw open the door, and pulled him inside.

In the brief flood of light, I saw shelves stacked with cleaning products and boxes of plastic gloves, a mop in a bucket in the corner. Then the door thudded shut behind us, choking the light, and there was nothing to see. Nothing to hear except the hitch of John's breath right before he kissed me again; nothing to feel except the solid bulk of his broad body against mine.

John nudged me up against the shelves with the patter of boxes jostling against each other. The steel frame pressed into my ass and my back, but I didn't give a shit, not when he was kissing me like there was nothing else in the entire universe.

I let go of his shirt to tease my hand up over his muscles beneath it. John let out a strangled groan and cupped my breast through my dress as he devoured my mouth. Pleasure raced over my skin with the sweep of his thumb over my nipple. I tweaked his nipples in turn, earning me a gasp. Then I let my hand slide all the way down to the waist of his pants.

I trailed my fingers over his fly, and his cock jumped beneath the thin fabric. "Fuck," John muttered against my mouth. He pulled back an inch, panting. "What are we doing, Jemma?"

"Being alive," I said firmly, and squeezed him as I stroked him through his pants. "Fuck me. Fuck me with all that life you've got in you."

A stuttered laugh escaped him, and his mouth crashed down on mine again. His hands traced down my sides and over my hips to the skirt of my dress. In one quick movement, he jerked the fabric up and caught my thighs. He lifted me against the shelves so my sex was flush against his groin.

I swallowed my moan as well as I could. If we were interrupted now, I just might kill someone.

John's mouth seared against my neck as he tugged my panties down, and I yanked at his fly. An ecstatic hum rumbled from his chest as I curled my fingers around his smooth hot length.

I'd lost track of my purse in the darkness. Every particle in my body resisted the idea of pulling apart to search for it. I'd trusted Sherlock without protection once. I trusted John just as much, didn't I? He wouldn't fuck me if he thought it would hurt me, not this sweet, good man.

He trusted me not to hurt him. Something stabbed deep down through me at that thought, but I shoved the emotion away. I wasn't going to hurt him right now. I was clean.

And oh God did I need him inside me right now.

If John had any doubts I hadn't expected, he didn't show them. His mouth reclaimed mine as the head of his cock slid against my wetness. He thrust into me so fast the bliss shot straight through my body and burst into stars behind my eyes.

We both knew we didn't have time for a leisurely roll in the hay. John bucked into me, one hand still clutching my thigh as he braced me against the shelf, the other on the shelf next to my shoulder to steady himself. I rocked to meet his thrusts, pleasure burning higher and farther with each jolt of our connection.

We *were* alive—alive and momentarily lost in it, in each other, in the ecstasy two bodies could make when they aligned in just the right way.

I felt John starting to lose control before I'd quite reached my peak, the jerks of his hips turning erratic. I growled with a hint of frustration against his lips, but his hand was already dipping between us to massage my clit. A fresh burst of pleasure flooded me with that touch, and I clenched around him with a swallowed cry. John buried his face in the crook of my neck to muffle a groan as he came with a spurt of heat.

We stayed there for a few moments, locked together in this hasty but incredibly intimate embrace, reluctant to return to the world waiting outside. But that world seeped back into my head even there in the dark where all I could taste and smell was the man softening inside me. It must have for John too. He withdrew with a ragged sigh.

There was so much pain in that sound in anticipation of the news we might hear when we ventured back into the waiting room. Hearing it, my lungs constricted. I snatched at my panties and straightened out my dress, but my stomach sank farther with each passing moment as the afterglow swiftly faded.

What had happened to Sherlock wasn't John's fault. I'd meant it when I'd said he wasn't his friend's keeper. But this, all of this, was *my* fault, wasn't it? I'd pulled these men into a conflict they could barely understand, and in doing so I'd made myself their keepers as the only one who could properly guide them.

And now my heart was wrenching at the thought of possibly losing one of them, nearly breaking at the possibility of another's pain on top of that.

I should have known better. I couldn't simply fuck my way through this problem. I couldn't scheme through it or power my way through it either. Somehow or other, I'd come to care about my London trio far too much. And now all of us might pay for it.

"Shall we get that dinner?" John said under his breath, a hint of amusement mingling with the strain in his voice. His hand found mine and squeezed it, making the ache inside me burrow deeper.

"I think we'd better, before someone wonders why we found this closet so interesting," I said, forcing a smile he couldn't see as much more my benefit as his.

We'd just returned to the waiting room after a lackluster meal when the doctor in charge of Sherlock's care appeared. John shot out of his chair in an instant.

"Your friend is recovering," the doctor said before he had to ask. "The drugs put a great strain in his body, and now he needs quiet and rest. He's awake at the moment— you can go in and see him, but one at a time, and no excitement, please."

John glanced at me as I got up, as if there was even any

question of who'd see Sherlock first. "Go on," I said. "Take as long as you need."

I followed him and the doctor down the hall and stopped outside the room. The doctor strode off, and John ducked inside. As I leaned against the wall to wait, I heard him take a harsh breath.

Sherlock's voice was thin but dry as ever. "You don't look terribly happy to see me, John."

John let out a sputter of a laugh. "I am. For God's sake, I was afraid you were going to die. I—you still don't look that far from it."

"I suppose that's a reasonable assessment, considering I don't feel far from it either."

My mouth twitched at the observation even as my throat tightened.

There was the scrape of a chair leg as John must have sat down. "I really don't know what I'd do with myself without you, you know," he said, so softly I barely made out the words.

Silence stretched for several seconds. Then Sherlock said, just as quietly, "I'm sorry. They were stronger than me."

John's voice turned fierce. "No, they weren't. You're still here, aren't you? Just... please don't give them another opportunity to come at you."

"I have certainly gained wisdom from this experience." Sherlock paused. "I meant to clear their influence from my mind. I wasn't trying to... leave. That isn't what I'd want either."

There was so much affection in his tone even if he couldn't bring himself to state his feelings more plainly. I lowered my head, my hands clenching.

I wasn't sure I'd be able to live with myself if I lost

another person who mattered to me because of my own carelessness, let alone someone who mattered so much to the other people in his life too. And regardless of wisdom gained, with the way the shrouded folk were ramping up their attacks, I might already be teetering on the edge of losing not just one but four.

Bash

The moment I opened the door for her, Jemma swept into my apartment like a hurricane. She stopped in the middle of the spartan living room and set her hands on her hips. "All right. Get all your things packed."

I stared at her for a moment, trying to read her mood in her taut expression. Her tone had been cool and matter-of-fact, but tension was woven through her body from feet to face like a bow stretched back to launch an arrow. I didn't think anyone would want to be in the way of that projectile when it flew.

"What's going on?" I asked, moving toward my bedroom where I had my small assortment of possessions that traveled with me. "What am I packing for?"

"Just get everything," Jemma said with a toss of her bright hair. "You won't be back here."

"Did something happen at the hospital? You said Sherlock came through all right." She'd said it in a voice oddly detached even for her, with barely any details other than the doctor was keeping him there for rest and observation for another day. Her monsters might have launched another attack since then.

Something flickered in her expression, so briefly I couldn't identify it. "He'll be fine. Not at his best for a little while, but—he survived. That's got nothing to do with this."

From the grit that flavored that last sentence, I had the feeling she wasn't being completely truthful. But I'd followed Jemma Moriarty an awful long way without always knowing exactly how or why she did the things she did, and she hadn't led us astray so far.

Most of my clothes were still in my suitcase from when I'd moved into the apartment a few weeks ago. I tossed in the few pieces that weren't already there, along with my electric razor and toothbrush, the western novel I was halfway through, my compact laptop, and... that was really about it. I already had my phone, wallet, and a pistol on me. A concealed pocket in the suitcase hid two other handguns.

"I'm sure you've got good reasons for this," I said as I rolled the suitcase into the living room. "I'd just appreciate knowing what they are. Or at least where we're going."

Jemma jerked her head toward the door. "I'll explain on the way. Come on."

Her car was parked outside. I tossed my suitcase in the back and got into the passenger seat. The engine roared as she took off like a shot. From the sugary smell that laced the air and the icing crumbs in the cup holder, she'd clearly downed a pastry or two on her way to get me.

Considering that we were in the middle of a mission that Jemma had appeared to be incredibly invested in, it didn't even occur to me that she might be moving me all the way out of London until she pulled up outside St. Pancras International train station. She turned off the engine and shifted in her seat to face me, pulling a leather men's wallet out of her purse.

"There's a credit card in here that you can use for a month or so and fifty thousand cash," she said in that same even voice. It might have actually gotten chilly now. "I want you to take the most direct route you can to Rome and wait for me there."

I took the wallet when she handed it to me, the leather smooth as my fingers closed around it. My stomach felt as if fingers had closed around it too. *A month or so.* "Are you staying here or going someplace else? How long do you expect it to take you to follow me?"

"I don't know yet. We'll see." She motioned to me with a flinty cast to her blue-gray eyes. "I know how to get in touch with you if I think it'll be longer than you can get by for on what I've given you."

She seemed to expect me to take off just like that. My entire body balked at the idea. Something about this scenario was totally wrong.

"This doesn't make sense," I said. "If you're staying here to take on Tillhouse and the commune he's allied with, you need me here with you. What the hell am I going to do in Rome?"

"Go shopping?" Jemma suggested with the most deadpan of humor. "Eat lots of pizza? I don't think you really got your fill last time."

"So this isn't a job. Mori, what the fuck is going on? You know I'll tackle whatever you need tackling. I've got to know what I'm dealing with first."

Jemma's mouth tightened. "It's a job because it's what

I'm ordering you to do—what I'm paying you to do. Because in case you've forgotten, I *am* your employer and you are my employee, and part of your job description is going where I tell you to go without asking a shitload of questions. So get going."

She spoke as steadily before, raising her chin at a haughty angle that raised my hackles automatically. My jaw clenched. "I might work for you, but we've been working *together* for seven years. We've been doing a hell of a lot more than working together the last few weeks. Shouldn't—"

"There isn't anything I should have to do," Jemma snapped, interrupting. "Get the fuck out of the car, Bash, and do as you're told—or you can consider yourself fired."

I might have stormed off then, licking my wounds and full of frustration I knew better than to throw back at her, except I noticed her hands in that moment. The one she'd set on her purse lay there easily enough, but she'd tucked the other close to her thigh. It had balled into a fist so tight the tendons stood out in her wrist.

She wasn't just tense—she was upset. And there weren't a whole lot of things in the world that could rattle Jemma Moriarty. This wasn't some cool-headed business decision; it was purely emotional.

Knowing where she'd come from, having been there when we'd found Sherlock, the pieces clicked into place way later than they really should have. She'd just taken me so much by surprise, which had probably been part of her plan in the first place. She'd known if she'd told me to pack before she'd gotten to the apartment, I'd have had more time to think through what was going on.

"Jemma," I said, quietly and calmly, "I'm not going. You are going to drive me back to my apartment, and I'm going to bring my things back up there, and we're going to raze these communes to the ground side-by-side. If that means you fire me, fine. I'll still be right there doing what I can whether you're paying me or not."

Her eyes narrowed, and she swallowed audibly. "Bash, I'm not playing around—"

"I know. And I'm not either. You know me well enough to figure out that I'm not going to run for the hills just because the going has gotten a little tough, don't you? No matter how mean you make yourself be about it."

She grimaced and jerked around in her seat. "Damn it."

Someone honked behind us. We'd been parked in the drop-off area for a few minutes now. With a growl of frustration, Jemma switched the engine back on and pulled away from the curb.

"Did you actually think that was going to work?" I asked.

"It seemed worth a try. You really are stubborn as a stack of concrete blocks."

I laughed at the mangled simile. "I'm pretty sure that's part of the reason you like me."

"Most of the time," she grumbled.

"Do you want to talk about it?"

"Not particularly."

She drove in silence the rest of the way back to my apartment, and I let her keep her own council. When we got there, though, she made no move to get out, as if she figured we could leave it just at that. I looked over at her, at this spectacular, brilliant, gorgeous woman I'd somehow managed to intertwine my life with, and a pang shot through my chest.

She was all of those things, but she was also still a

human being, even if she sometimes didn't quite believe that. Even if I sometimes forgot it too.

"Come up with me," I said. "Please."

She met my gaze with a little surprise. I didn't normally bother with a lot of politeness, but I'd figured it would get her attention.

"I *don't* really want to talk about it," she said.

"Fine. There are a few things I'd like to talk about. Will you listen to me?"

She wavered, and then a little of the tension seeped out of her posture. "Yeah, I can do that."

Jemma even looked a little apologetic as I hauled my suitcase back of the stairs to the fourth floor, because none of these old buildings in central London had elevators. I chucked it in my bedroom and returned to Jemma where she was standing in the middle of the living room. The urge came over me to just hold her, to take some of the weight she was obviously carrying, but I didn't think that was what she needed. She was trying so very fucking hard to be the strongest person in the world right now.

"I'll admit it, okay?" I said. "I'm sure your monsters have been working their voodoo on me too. I've had dreams—I've been more on edge—but I have it under control. If you think I'm crossing a line, you go right ahead and smack me one. Until then, I know you're not trying to send me away for *your* benefit, so it's obviously supposed to be for mine."

"You don't know for sure that they won't push you farther than you're prepared to handle sometime when I'm not around to intervene," Jemma said. "If we'd gotten to Sherlock even a half hour later, he'd probably be dead right now."

"So what? That's the risk we all decided to take when we signed on."

"But you didn't really understand that risk." She flung her hands out into the air. "I can tell you things until I'm blue in the face, but you can't really comprehend what the shrouded folk are like, what they're capable of, until you experience it. *I* didn't even know everything they were capable of, and I lived with the fiends for fourteen years. I meant to do this on my own when I was first planning things out. I shouldn't have gotten you as mixed up in it as I did. It's my responsibility, no one else's."

"Hey." I did walk right up to her then, setting my hands on her shoulders and catching her gaze. "You've warned us as much as you could every step of the way. I have the right to make whatever decision I want with that information. I want to be here with you. I don't give a fuck what kind of danger it puts me in. I'd rather die seeing out your mission than live eating pizza in Rome while you battle on alone here. Don't you know *that* by now?"

She gave me a crooked grin, but she didn't look away. "Maybe I did and I was just hoping I was wrong."

"Mori…" I let out a breath. Part of me wanted to tell her that while she wasn't getting rid of *me*, if she wanted me to cut her trio out of our operation, all she had to do was say the word and I'd make sure they never set another foot near her or the shrouded folk. The words halted halfway up my throat.

Making that offer would only turn me into a massive hypocrite. If I could believe I was going to do her more good than harm by sticking with her, I had to admit the three of them probably would too.

"The same applies to the others," I said, "if you were planning on trying to scare them off too. They've got the right to make their own informed decision—and I think it's pretty clear what decision they're set on."

Jemma lowered her head. "I didn't mean for things to turn out like this when we first came to London. I didn't mean for any of this to happen. It's gotten so... complicated."

"Maybe in some ways. In other ways, I've found it's letting me see how simple certain facts are." I paused, holding in the other words I'd wanted to say more than once, the words that had probably been true for years now if I'd let myself examine my emotions more closely.

If a man who'd barely known her a few months could say it, why the fuck couldn't I?

I eased a little closer, one of my hands coming up to tease into her hair. "I never said this before because I thought you wouldn't want to hear it, but maybe I should have trusted you more than that. You are the meaning in my life. You may as well make the sun rise. I don't want to exist if it's not beside you. You are *never* getting rid of me, because I love you too goddamned much to ever let you go."

She raised her eyes to stare at me. "Bash..."

I stroked my fingers over her fiery hair. "I mean it. I love you. God only knows how long I have."

Her voice came out low and hoarse. "I don't know if I'm ever going to be able to say that back to anyone. I think that part of me died when my sister did."

I smiled at her, at the woman I loved with every fiber of my being, and said with totally honesty. "I don't really give a damn whether you ever return the sentiment. I'll fight with you and rise or fall with you anyway. 'The course of true love never did run smooth.' Shakespeare was right about a few things. Let's just hope we get a little more rise before the fall."

CHAPTER TWENTY-ONE

Jemma

The stretch of land around Tillhouse's country cottage was far too open for my liking. Just a broad field with overgrown grass dotted with wildflowers. I lingered for a moment in the shelter of the grove of trees on the other side of the worn wooden fence before clambering over and slipping across the yard.

In the light of a quarter moon, I could only make out the broader details of the small stone building. No vehicles were parked outside, and no light glinted in any of the windows. By all appearances, I shouldn't run into anyone during this operation. The cuff clamped around my thigh should stop any shrouded folk lingering around from noticing me too.

A twinge ran through the muscle there as I stopped near the side of the building. I'd been wearing the cuff more than I preferred the last few days—and my body obviously wasn't very happy about that fact either. But I couldn't risk tipping off Tillhouse or the local cultists before I had a new plan in place for taking them on.

I leaned against the cool stone and peered through the window beside me. Nothing but shadows waited on the other side. I stood still, my ears perked, but the only sound that reached me was the faint rustling of the night breeze over the grass.

Setting my feet carefully and quietly, I walked around to the back door. Even when the house's surroundings were totally open like they were here, people so often focused their security on the front door as if it were more vulnerable than the others.

Tillhouse intended to keep this place as impenetrable as he could, though. A glance through the window in the door showed me the red gleam of a light on an electronic security system. I could just barely make out the company name. It was one of those where you had to type in the right code to disarm it within a certain number of seconds or the authorities would be alerted.

Too bad for Tillhouse I'd come prepared. I slipped the device Bash had picked up for me out of my purse and kept it tucked under my arm as I went to work on the keyhole. It hadn't been hard to figure out what kind of security breaker I might need after I'd already penetrated Tillhouse's office and London apartment. Most people found one company they trusted and stuck with that one across the board.

It was those investigations that had led me here. I'd found a piece of mail addressed to a nearby PO Box that had fallen behind the sofa in his apartment. Tracking down the name it'd been addressed to had brought up the deed for this cottage. No actual person with that name appeared to exist, so it was almost certainly an alias. For some reason, Tillhouse didn't want anyone to easily connect him to this Yorkshire property.

I was hoping that reason would pay off with enough information to get me to my final goal.

The lock clicked over. I paused, adjusting my headset. "How does it look out there?" I asked under my breath.

Bash was staked out in our car a few miles down the road—the only road that had access to the lane that led to this cottage. "All clear so far," he said in my ear. "You know I'll alert you the second I see anything at all."

"Okay. I'm going in."

I eased open the door and darted across the tiled floor to the security panel. The plastic side popped open as the system beeped in warning of impending doom. I plugged the breaker device into a port there and jabbed a few buttons on its face.

The beeping stopped, the pane on the security panel going dark. I let out a sigh of relief and unplugged the device.

Even though the place was isolated and Tillhouse was a busy man, he must have made a point of getting out here on a fairly regular basis. The inside of the building had an airy flowery scent, not at all stuffy from being shut up. The floor turned to hardwood as I left the back hall, my shoes rasping softly over its surface.

Sherlock probably would have jumped at the chance to join this search. Breaking and entering was one of his favorite activities, as far as I could tell. I'd bet John would have been thrilled too. But Sherlock had still looked a little pale and shaky when I'd seen him this morning, and frankly, I hadn't needed any of them to pull this off.

It was a return to form—me and Bash working alone, making do with the extensive resources we'd accumulated for just this purpose. Perhaps it'd be nearly as difficult to put off the trio as it'd been with Bash, but that didn't mean I had to involve them in all of my activities. I could include them in moderation, keep them out of the riskier situations. Take a larger share of the responsibility that should have been completely mine.

I took a quick turn through the kitchen, not expecting the old-fashioned appliances and stylishly shabby wooden table to reveal much. Living rooms often proved more useful, but the one here didn't offer a single scrap of paper or telling photograph. Onward to the bedroom, then.

A faint scent reached my nose as I entered that small room—something flat and prickly like an herb left to dry too long. I couldn't place it exactly, but my pulse sped up at the smell with some memory beyond my consciousness. I peered through the darkened room intently as I started my search.

After several minutes, it appeared that initial spark of anticipation had been misleading. The wardrobe held only folded sweaters and polo shirts and a row of hanging slacks. Nothing was hidden under the mattress or behind the headboard. I was stepping back with a frown when my gaze caught on a scuffing on the floor just beneath the bed.

The varnish on the hardwood was worn down quite a bit by the legs of the bed—as if it'd regularly been pushed to the north side of the room. Bracing myself for the squeal of metal against wood, I positioned my hands and gave the whole frame a good shove.

It moved about a foot on my first attempt—far enough to reveal a line of slightly thicker shadow in the floor. There was a trap door under the bed. My lips curled into a grin. Jackpot.

I pushed the bed until it was far enough over that I could tug the trap door open. A cooler darkness waited below, laced with a stronger whiff of that herbal scent. I pulled out my phone and shone its light into the depths.

A ladder led down some eight feet into the cellar. Most of the floor was covered by a rug. A chair and table small enough to fit through the trap door stood in one corner, and a metal shelving unit that must have been constructed down there stood against the opposite wall.

Clutching my phone, I clambered down the ladder one-handed. The cool, prickly-smelling air closed around me.

Tillhouse wasn't likely to have communed with the shrouded folk down here. They hesitated to go anywhere underground, away from the sunlight. But opening the boxes on the shelf, I found a variety of artifacts he might have used in his own sort of worship elsewhere.

A blood-stained silk cloth told me he'd participated in the bloodletting ceremony at least once. He had several of the wood-and-wire tokens that the cult often sold to supernatural enthusiasts. Apparently the shrouded folk and their human devotees hadn't been upfront enough with the MP to inform him that those objects held no power or significance at all. He was a dupe just like the other collectors, just in a much more involved way.

That didn't endear Tillhouse to me at all, but it did make me even more nervous about what the shrouded folk might be planning to use him for.

The contents of the next box sent a jitter of excitement through me. He'd made notes about the commune—he'd even drawn maps. Maybe he'd duped the cult in turn. They wouldn't have approved of him having this information written down anywhere outside their domain.

One piece of paper, with multiple eraser marks as if he'd been drawing from memory, showed the layout of some twenty buildings in what must have been the commune itself. Another marked its spot about halfway between two town names I recognized from our Highlands investigations.

We had them. We knew exactly where they were now. It didn't matter if Tillhouse had gotten off the hook—when we destroyed his local base of support, he wouldn't matter anyway.

Unable to hold back a smile, I snapped pictures of both maps with my phone. Part of me wanted to get the hell out of that tight dark space as soon as possible, but my practical side won out. There were still a few more boxes I hadn't checked yet. I hadn't come all this way to rush through the job.

The next container held another assortment of knickknacks. I set that back in the spot where I'd found it and then reached for another. This one lifted in my hands with much less jostling.

It held a stack of papers. I shone my light over the sheets as I flipped through them. It only took a scan of the first few before a cold knot of horror began to swell in my gut.

The papers held notes about diversions of funds, about arranging access to supplies, about coordinating worship ceremonies… not just within the Highlands commune or between it and the other two here, but with ones noted down as *Colorado* and *Arizona*, *Granada* and *Luzern*.

If I was interpreting the figures here correctly, the shrouded folk here in Britain had turned Tillhouse into some sort of hub, connecting them with other pockets of the cult all across North America and Europe so they could collaborate more closely than they'd ever been able to from their isolated locations. Fuck.

While I'd been gathering power to take them on, they'd been gathering more power themselves, for who knew what awful purpose.

Nausea pooled in my stomach as I took photos of all the papers in the box for further examination. I climbed back up the ladder on legs that had gone slightly shaky. My head had just emerged from the level of the floor when Bash's voice crackled into my ear.

"—there? Jemma, if you don't answer me right now—"

"I'm here," I said quickly. "What's happening?" The cellar depths must have cut off the signal between us.

"A motorcycle went by about thirty seconds ago. I don't know for sure they're heading to your spot, but I'm not sure where else they'd be going. You'd better get out of there."

I swore under my breath and flipped the trap door closed. I couldn't leave the house looking like someone had poked around in it. With a massive heave, I hauled the bed back into its previous spot. Then I fled for the back door.

When I darted out into the yard, a headlight was just streaking around the bend by the stand of trees. I ran in the opposite direction so the building would hide any sight of me and threw myself down into the tall grass about fifty feet away.

The light stopped by the lane. In its hazy glow, I saw the helmeted figure on the bike turn their head as if scanning the area. Not Tillhouse, but someone he hired to keep a watch on the place? I might have been safer staying inside.

After a few minutes, the bike roared off again. My muscles went slack against the firm ground. I rubbed my eyes and patted my phone to make sure I hadn't lost it somehow in my rush to get out.

"Bash," I said into my headpiece, "we're going to need to round up and rally the trio."

Everything revolved around that commune in the Highlands. We had to take it down as swiftly and decisively as possible if we were going to actually put an end to this, and for that five minds and bodies would get us a lot farther than two.

CHAPTER TWENTY-TWO

John

"I'm sorry, Mr. Holmes," the commander of the North Highland police said for what felt like the hundredth time. He folded his hands on his desk. "There isn't much we can do for you. I understand you have quite a reputation that proceeds you, but we still must follow proper procedure if we're to keep law and order."

Sherlock's lips pursed as if he'd bitten into something bitter, but he kept his voice as even as always. "I realize that. I simply wish to gain access to your historical records so that we might establish a pattern—"

"And I've told you that those records aren't available to the public. As much as you may have helped the police down in London and wherever else, you don't work for *us*, and none of your friends here do either. I'm afraid that's my final answer."

I could tell Sherlock was biting his tongue, but the drawn-out argument had clearly worn at him. He'd been more his usual color when we'd struck out on our mission this morning after a night in a nearby inn, but since then his face had started to gray. At the moment, it was unsettlingly close to the shade it'd been when he'd first gotten out of the hospital. My stomach twisted, and I resisted the urge to glare at the police commander for bringing my partner to that state.

Garrett had changed colors too—an angry flush, in his case. "Fuck," he muttered as we left the building and headed to the van where Jemma and Bash were waiting. The long-time criminals in our midst had figured it was better not to put on an appearance for the local constabulary.

"Do you think Tillhouse has some influence over them to make them so reluctant to share information?" I asked Sherlock. I'd never seen any body of law enforcement be so hesitant to help the great Sherlock Holmes.

"It could be. Or perhaps there are paranormal vibes in the air." He made a swishing gesture in the air and closed his hand when it trembled. "It could also simply be the northern Scottish dislike of most things English. Our history with them is not the most cordial, after all."

Well, yes, there was that too. Maybe the simplest explanation applied here.

Jemma took in our faces as we climbed into the van and wrinkled her nose. "No luck then?"

"The North Highland police force take the privacy of their records very seriously," Sherlock announced, and immediately sat down on one of the padded benches that lined the walls. It'd only been a few days. I wasn't sure his recovery was quite complete. He'd have denied any weakness, of course.

I sank down beside him, and Jemma shoved the box of donuts she'd bought on our way up toward us as if as a consolation prize, licking her fingers from her latest snack. Even though my gut was heavy, I picked up a salted caramel one. Sweets always seemed to sharpen her concentration. It could be worth a try.

The sticky caramel dissolved into the buttery dough as I chewed. I wasn't sure the sugar rush jostled loose any useful inspirations, but I did have to say that Jemma had excellent taste in desserts.

"Why don't we approach this the same way we did the place in the Lake District?" Bash asked where he'd turned around in the front passenger seat. His dark gaze passed over us, slightly narrowed as if he was annoyed the three of us hadn't already gotten to work on it. "Set them up for a crime, then send the police to catch them. It went off without a hitch before."

Jemma shook her head with a swish of her red waves across her shoulders. "We haven't gotten any bites for the feelers I put out, just as I suspected. We gambled on that first attempt to get Tillhouse arrested, and now they'll be on high alert. I doubt the commune will react to any bait we dangle—for now, they'll be sticking to people they're sure of."

"They might not need anything from the outside world," Sherlock put in. "With Tillhouse contributing extra supplies to whatever stores they usually kept, they may be keeping themselves set up for months at a time."

"That can't be the end of it," Garrett protested, but he hesitated when he looked at Sherlock. The overdose had clearly shaken him up too. He hadn't been quite his usual passionate, quick-tempered self since we'd discovered Sherlock unconscious. I got the impression he was afraid if he came on too strong about anything, he'd accidentally trigger some unknown sensitivity in the other man.

We'd all relied on Sherlock an awful lot over the past few years. He'd almost come to seem like a god of detection and deduction. That evening last week had been a horrible reminder of just how mortal and human the man was.

I'd flushed the rest of Sherlock's cocaine down the loo before he'd gotten home, and he hadn't complained, so I'd won at least that minor victory.

Jemma snatched up another donut and leaned back against the bench. "I still say we could take the slaughtering route. Toss some hydrochloric gas into the place. Electrocute them all. I don't care. Just get rid of them, and goodbye problem." She waved her hand.

I'd have liked to say I was horrified by her suggestion and by the fact that I suspected she honestly would have been fine with simply killing every inhabitant of the Highlands commune. The truth was, after the wrenching shock of finding Sherlock slumped in his bedroom and the agonizing hours waiting to find out if he'd even survive, I couldn't summon much if any compassion for the people who'd welcomed the creatures who'd tormented him.

No, a large part of me wouldn't mind seeing them tormented just as much in return.

I did still have a conscience, though. And there were practical concerns as well.

"You commit a mass murder, and there'll be a huge investigation," Garrett said. "I'd rather not stake my career on the police up here being too stupid to put together the evidence." He sighed and grabbed a donut for himself. "It's too bad these commune arseholes don't take the same route as plenty of other cults and mass suicide themselves."

At his words, an idea sparked in my head so abruptly and insistently that I looked at Sherlock, assuming if I'd thought of it, the same thing must have occurred to him even faster. But he was gazing toward the van's tinted window with an expression that was either thoughtful or dazed, depending on how generous you were being.

I waffled for a few seconds. If the possibility *hadn't* occurred to him, it probably wasn't a good one. I might be better off keeping my mouth shut. But maybe he hadn't even registered Garrett's remark, deep in his own contemplations.

If he and Garrett didn't have the best grip on themselves, then *someone* out of the three of us needed to keep us on track.

I wet my lips. "What if… what if we made it *look* like they did it to themselves? A mass suicide?"

Sherlock's head jerked around. He blinked at me. "Are you seriously suggesting we murder all those people?"

"No!" I said quickly, to Jemma's amused smirk. "I was thinking—we can't get them to take the bait for an actual crime. We're not sure we could convince the authorities to go after them if we simply make one up. But while the police force is hesitant to pin the locals with a crime, especially one we're presenting them with, they're a lot more likely to rush in if it's to help, aren't they? We find a way to call them in so they'll find the cultists unconscious but not yet dead—so there's still time for medical treatment."

Sherlock raised his eyebrows. "And how exactly would that play out, as you're seeing it?"

Under his scrutiny, my instinct was to bite my tongue. The idea was on the table now, and he still wasn't jumping on it, so how viable could it be?

Then I thought of the graying of his face and the tremble of his hand, and resolve hardened inside me.

Jemma's voice from our talk in the hospital echoed up from my memory. *You're more than just his goddamned sidekick. How many people did you save before you even met him?*

She was right. I had to give myself more credit—starting right now. Sherlock didn't have all the answers, and I shouldn't expect him to. Maybe it was all that pressure that had pushed him over the edge, even if mainly from himself.

I glanced at Bash, who was watching me with evident curiosity. "You have military contacts, don't you? On the black market side of things? There are a couple of different gases that contain chemicals people could have taken by other means, and that would give us enough of a window between knocking the cultists out and them actually dying for a rescue team to come in and get to work."

Jemma's eyes glittered with eager understanding. "We set them up to look like they've done the whole suicide pact thing. Stick cups in their hands with residue of the same chemicals, that sort of thing. That's what you're thinking?"

Her approval gave me a renewed burst of confidence. "Exactly. We could drag out some of the most egregious evidence of their crimes too—we could plant some obvious things related to Tillhouse to tie him into the whole mess and, er, kill two birds with one stone."

Sherlock's gaze had gone distant again but in a more intent way. It shifted to me after a moment.

"You're sure about this, John?" he said. "The use of the gas wouldn't be evident? We wouldn't end up with a few dozen deaths on our hands?"

"This is my area of expertise," I reminded him. "I treated soldiers who'd inhaled one thing or another in the field. It's not a common tactic anymore, but it's still used frequently enough and in much more variety than before that we can pick our materials to suit our ends. Most of the modern forms disperse quite quickly. It won't be hard to time, either. We can alert the authorities before we even douse the place, wait until we know the emergency vehicles are close enough."

Jemma made a derisive sound as if she didn't much care whether we saved the people, which she probably didn't. I ignored that. Garrett had leaned forward on the bench, his usual energy back in his stance.

"And if there's enough evidence of suicide and their general insanity, no one's going to be looking for evidence that it was anything else. It'll be a simple case, cut and dried. They'd be able to say whatever they wanted about their supposed innocence and no one would believe it was an attack."

A slow, grim smile crept across Bash's face. "I have the contacts to get whatever we need," he said in his low voice. "Give me a list, and I can have it within a day or two."

That was barely any time at all. My heart skipped a beat at the thought of the course I was launching us into.

A hint of a smile had touched even Sherlock's face. He clapped me on the shoulder with a glint of emotion in his pale blue eyes that flared a little hotter than just admiration.

"It sounds as though you've hit on just the thing, my dear Watson. Let's get to work, then."

Even though the course I'd just set us on terrified me, I had to grin back.

CHAPTER TWENTY-THREE

Jemma

Now that I'd tackled a few of these communes, I could predict where the guards would be stationed with great accuracy. Between my stealth, my night vision goggles, and the element of surprise, it didn't take me very long to dispatch each of them before they could give the slightest warning.

The last of the guards crumpled from my arms. I jerked back the syringe I'd used to dose him, shoved that into my bag, and arranged his body with a chemical-laced cup a few inches from his limp hand. Then I touched the button on my mic.

"They're all down," I murmured to the four men waiting in the van farther off. My gaze settled on the distant shadows up the slope between the trees where I knew the main commune lay, just beneath the mountain's peak. Some night creature rustled in the brush, and I tensed instinctively, the cool, fresh Highlands air rushing into my lungs.

It wouldn't be so fresh in a few minutes. "We're coming in with the gas," John said.

Bash's voice followed. "I'll meet up with you in the commune. All suited up and ready to go."

The two of us were going to be laying out our evidence in the settlement. I reached for my own gas mask, procured via one of Bash's ex-military contacts.

A pale shape swooped between the trees up ahead, and my pulse hiccupped. It was probably only an owl, but the image triggered too many associations deep in my brain. Olivia with her pale blond hair, spinning in a white dress. Olivia running between the stunted trees around the commune *we'd* called home.

A chill much sharper than the one in the air dug into my skin. Shit. I hadn't even thought.

My hand paused with my gas mask against my chest. "John," I whispered. "The dose you're going to be giving them all—it's enough to bring down an adult. What about the kids?"

The hesitation on the other end made my heart thud faster. When we were thinking of the cult is a bunch of sadistic demon worshippers, people who'd been indirectly responsible for Sherlock's near death, it was easy to forget the innocents among them. I had no idea how many children might be in this commune, but I had to assume there'd be at least a few. The shrouded folk demanded their sacrifices.

"I picked the levels carefully," the former doctor said. "It should be just enough to knock out a big guy, but not so much it'd do immediate damage even to someone small. They should be all right."

Should be. That wasn't enough of a guarantee for my

liking. I yanked the mask up over my face and hurried through the forest toward the commune.

If anyone died tonight, it'd be the right people, at least this once.

A mist started streaming through the woods from where the guys must have parked. I picked up my pace, my breath muggy inside the gas mask. If this commune operated like the others I'd known did, I'd have a tiny window between the point when the adults had fallen and when the kids might be in danger. I just had to make it there in time.

Someone coughed in the distance. Someone else let out a shout of warning. It was too late for them. Most of the commune would have been sleeping at this hour, sucked even deeper under by the chemical cocktail, but the few who'd been on watch right in the settlement hadn't stood a chance either. The thumps of their bodies hitting the ground reached my ears a few seconds later.

I outright ran then, not bothering to worry about the crunch of twigs or the rattle of pebbles under my feet. The rough wooden buildings came into view, Bash's brawny form moving among them. He bent down to shift a body and place one of our doctored cups.

I raised a hand in acknowledgement as I dashed past him and spun around to scan the settlement's erratic layout. They tried to avoid any sort of pattern that might disturb the shrouded folk in planning the placement of their buildings, but they had other patterns of inhabitation. Usually the kids slept in one of the north buildings…

Or rather, under one of the north buildings. I threw open one door, scanned the floor, rushed to the next, and spotted the half-open trap door beside a bed where the two cultists on "parental" duty were sprawled in their beds.

The gas was already seeping through that opening into the dug-out basement room where the younger members of the cult spent their nights. The close quarters and uncomfortable surroundings gave them more motivation to harass each other for the shrouded folk's pleasure, and the door was always left partly open so the adults could hear if any conflict became too violent. Now it could spell their doom.

A small voice was coughing below, another whimpering. I dropped down by the door and leaned my face to the opening. I couldn't make out more than a few huddled outlines of small bodies, but the fragility of even that sight was enough to constrict my chest.

When the cops came, they'd be saved. They'd be placed with real families, families that wouldn't offer them up in bloody worship. I was saving them right now.

"Stay here," I told them in a voice muffled by my gas mask. "Don't come out until you hear footsteps coming in up here. Then you can yell for them to get you. Do you understand?"

"Yes," a thin voice murmured, and coughed again. "Who *are* you?"

I smiled behind the mask. "A guardian angel," I said, and shoved the trap door shut.

If the kids reported my arrival to the police or the emergency workers, they'd assume the gas had made them hallucinate an angel. That suited me just fine. I yanked a blanket off one of the slumped forms and spread it over the trap door to seal it even more from the gas. Then I jerked at the adults' bodies and set them up with their own drugged cups.

When I emerged, Bash was just coming out of another of the buildings, his face disguised by his mask. He motioned to his duffel bag, and I nodded. With swift efficiency, we unrolled the banner we'd made, the letters painted with chicken's blood, and strung it between two of the trees.

In honor of our great provider, Harvey Tillhouse, we offer up our spirits. We'd even pasted a photograph of the MP on there for good measure.

We raced through the commune, setting up the rest of the bodies, scattering our additional evidence. Notes of gratitude and more photos of the MP here. The tools of the blood-letting and other torture there. No one who walked through this place would be able to deny something deeply sick had caught hold of these people.

Sherlock's voice carried into my ear. "The police should be arriving in approximately five minutes. A couple of news teams too. Complete your work and hurry out of there."

I was just laying the last finishing touches around one of the fallen guards. We also wanted the reporters we'd tipped off to have plenty of sensational material to capture with their cameras. Tillhouse could deny all he wanted, but he couldn't stop the public commotion that would follow. No one was going to vote for a man known to associate with suicide cults.

I caught Bash's eye in a brief acknowledgement, and we took off in our respective directions. He was leaving with the guys, and I'd taken my own small car to arrive here a little ahead of them. We'd meet up back at the hotel in a couple hours.

The breeze was already dispersing the gas. It teased

through my hair as I tugged off my mask. I held the bulky thing under my arm and loped on.

My thigh muscle was prickling beneath the gold cuff around my leg by the time I reached the little navy blue car. I grimaced as I hopped in, tossing my stuff on the passenger seat, but I didn't want to take the cuff off until I was well away.

The prickling expanded into an ache as I drove off down the narrow lane. The road wove back and forth through the trees down the mountain slope, with enough bumps that my stomach started to churn. I gripped the steering wheel tighter and focused on breathing evenly.

We'd done it. The commune would be shattered, Tillhouse's career would be upended—the shrouded folk couldn't possibly counteract the mess we'd just set in motion. And with that shattering, all those connections they'd been building in their international network would fray too.

The UK was clear now. Where to next? I'd have liked to tackle the fiends on my home ground now, but it'd be easier for the trio to follow me to continental Europe instead. If they were going to follow me. I'd kept in mind what Bash had said about letting them make their own decisions, and they *had* pulled this last desperate gambit off...

The pain in my thigh jabbed all the way to the bone. I flinched, my foot jerking against the gas pedal and nearly shooting me off the edge of a bend.

I managed to slam on the brake instead. The pain seared deeper as I caught my breath. It looked like I didn't have a choice about this anymore.

I yanked up the parking brake and fumbled with my pant leg as quickly as I could. The second I'd snapped the cuff off, the pain dissipated. I sagged back in the seat, waiting while the muscle gradually unclenched and the adrenaline of the moment washed away. My eyes drifted closed just for a moment.

When I opened them, a pale filmy figure was floating just beyond the windshield.

A startled squeak slipped from my throat before I could catch it. The shrouded one loomed closer, streaming its strips of faded cloth or skin or whatever that was. My hand reached for the gear shift instinctively, but if the fiend was going to try to fuck me over, maybe it was better if I wasn't operating a moving vehicle.

I rolled down the window, the cold night air flooding the car's interior. "What do you want?" I said in my flattest voice.

The shrouded one drifted around to the window, its dark void of a face even more impenetrable than the thickest shadows in the forest around us. Looking at it sent a shiver through my chest to my gut.

"You are the one that escaped the contract," it said in the dry, distant tone it shared with all the shrouded folk I'd heard speak.

I didn't see any point in denying that fact. "I am. What's your point?"

"I have a message for you. You will stop your interference, or your sister will die."

I stared at the thing until a hysterical laugh burst from my throat. "You're a little too late with that threat. My sister has been dead for years."

"She is not. She was taken but not consumed. And the one who took her wants you to stand down."

"Yeah, right. Forgive me if I don't believe you just because you said so. I'll keep doing whatever the hell I feel like doing, thank you very much." The shrouded folk didn't kidnap people and then keep them alive for years. They seared them down to their souls and swallowed them whole.

The gauzy figure wavered. A small wooden box appeared amid its flowing strips. "The one who has her sends proof. The decision is yours. Make one more move against our supporters, and there will be much blood spilled that you'd rather avoid."

It flung the box through the open window. The container dropped onto the passenger seat. When I glanced back toward the shrouded one, it had already vanished.

My stomach clenched tight. I reached for the box tentatively, half afraid simply touching it would hurt me somehow. But it felt like plain, solid wood.

I held it in front of me and popped the lid open. My whole body froze.

Lying on a bed of cotton in the middle of the box was a severed toe, so fresh it was leaking blood into the fabric.

CHAPTER TWENTY-FOUR

Jemma

There were too many goddamned birds twittering outside the window. I tugged the pane shut with a thump, even though it was a hot morning in the Highlands and the farmhouse Bash and I had rented didn't have any air conditioning.

After the window was closed, I gazed out it down the lane that wove between the two nearby slopes and disappeared beyond them. In the summer sunlight, the grass shone emerald green.

Bash came in with two cups of coffee. With only a brief glance away from the window, I leaned forward in the chair to accept one from him. I inhaled the steam before taking a sip. He'd put nearly the right amount of sugar in, enough that it cut through the bitterness to tingle over my tongue.

"No sign of it yet?" he said.

I shook my head. "Delivery is supposed to be by nine

am. Someone's getting their ear shouted off if it doesn't turn up in ten minutes."

I made the comment wryly, but every part of my body was wound up in anticipation. I didn't know whether I was more afraid that the test would show I'd been told the truth or lied to. Both options were exceptionally horrific in their differing ways.

Bash lowered himself onto the edge of the bed next to my chair. "Assuming it's nothing—assuming it was just one of the monsters' sick mind games—you're thinking Spain next?"

"From the notes, it looks like the one commune there is larger than any we've dealt with here. I think it'd be a good next step."

"And we'd be looping your Londoners back in, or going it alone?"

"Do you really think they'd let me off the hook after all that?" I raised my eyebrows at him. "We're lucky we didn't get more argument about this little retreat."

I'd told the trio that I needed a few days of space to work out a few things before we continued our mission against the shrouded folk. Then I'd taken every possible caution to make sure the rental of this house *couldn't* be traced to me, just in case they got nosy, as had happened before. You couldn't be too careful with Sherlock Holmes in the mix.

At the growl of a motor, my back tensed even more than it already had been. A white car with a courier logo came into view on the lane. I stood up. My heart beat out a staccato rhythm at the base of my throat.

Bash got up too, watching me. "Do you want me there with you when you open it?"

I turned the idea over in my head as the car sped

toward the house. "No. I think I'd like to be completely alone to work out what I'm going to make of the result before I have to figure out anything else."

He inclined his head and sat back down as I headed for the stairs.

The knock came just as I reached the pastel yellow front hall. I signed with the fake name I'd given the company and accepted the thick envelope with a stiff smile. Then I sat down in the living room and waited until the sound of the car's engine had faded away.

The envelope's seal tore easily. I slid the papers out, and my hand trembled. I'd sent away a little of my blood and a little from the severed toe the shrouded one had so graciously gifted me with to a DNA testing facility with an extra fee for expedited results. As I looked down at the plain type printed across the stiff paper, my mouth went dry.

Analyzing the submitted samples... The results are conclusive to a high degree of validity... The two samples are a high enough match to indicate shared parentage.

My fingers twitched. The paper slipped from them. As it drifted to the floor, I stared at my empty hand.

No shrouded folk hallucination could have faked that result. A digit severed years ago wouldn't have been seeping fresh blood. My parents, if they were even still alive, couldn't have had any other children—I remembered my mother complaining about the hot flashes of her menopause a few years before I'd fled.

It was true. Olivia was alive. She was still *alive*. Oh my God.

A rush of adrenaline hit me, joy and anger mixed together. I hadn't failed her after all. I still had a chance to save her. What the hell had the folk being doing with her all this fucking time?

She hadn't been at my old commune when I'd gone back for her. Everyone there had believed she'd been taken in sacrifice. Which meant she hadn't been kept in this world. The shrouded folk had dragged her off to their own horrible realm. The tortures she must have endured—when I got my hands on their floating mummified asses—

The ring of my phone interrupted my silent tirade. I fished it out and frowned at the unknown number. It was the phone I'd used with the trio, but the caller wasn't in my contacts. I hesitated and then answered it.

"Hello?"

"Miss Moriarty." Sherlock's measured voice carried over the slightly staticky connection. "I'm glad you're up on this fine morning. Would you mind if I dropped in for a visit?"

He'd called from a different phone because he'd suspected I wouldn't answer if I'd known for sure it was him. I made a grimace he couldn't see. "I'm a little occupied at the moment, and I'm still out of town. Believe me, as soon as I'm ready to pick up the quest again, I'll let you know."

"Funny thing. I don't entirely believe you. You have been in the habit of giving us the slip. Which is why I'm currently at a hotel about a half hour's drive from that house you've taken up residence in. The Highlands rather appealed to you, did they?"

My chest tightened. He was up *here*? He knew where we were staying? Or perhaps it was a gambit to try to get the information out of me. "Nice try."

"Surely you have more faith in my investigative abilities than that by now." He rattled off the house's name and address. My stomach sank. "You employed some worthy tricks, Jemma, but I've come to know you quite well. No more sneaking off on us. Whatever you're occupied with, I want to hear about it—until those creatures we're battling are wiped off the face of this earth."

An admirable and absolutely frustrating sentiment. I closed my eyes and dragged in a slow breath.

This wasn't going to work. He wouldn't understand—the lengths I'd need to go to if I meant to rescue my sister—the trio wouldn't just stand by for that. They'd say I was taking things too far or that I shouldn't go it alone, blunder in with all their good intentions and ignorance of the shrouded folk… They'd insist on interfering like he was right now, and that could easily ruin everything. If I was going to reach Olivia, I had to keep a perfect balance of elements they barely comprehended.

I'd gotten back my chance to save my sister. To keep the promise I'd made to her ten years ago. To make up for leaving her behind to the tortures of our commune while I made my escape.

I couldn't put that mission at risk, not in the slightest way. If I failed her *again* because I couldn't keep these over-enthusiastic men at bay…

"John accompanied me, of course," Sherlock was saying into my silence. "Garrett should be up this evening for the weekend. That job of his does get in the way more often than not, as useful as I suppose it often is."

"So the gang will all be here," I said, willing my voice to stay steady. "Wonderful." *What could I do to make you leave again?*

Nothing. Not as long as they had working minds and bodies. Not as long as they believed I was still working on the most pressing problem the world had ever faced. If I could be sure of getting even a week without Sherlock tracking me down all over again… But he was far too stubborn for that, wasn't he? Far too stubborn, far too brilliant, and now he'd had far too much time to observe my habits in ways I couldn't be fully aware of.

The answer rose up in my head with cold certainty. My throat constricted, but I didn't shy away from the thought. I studied it in its brutal clarity, the gears in my mind already whirring with their usual sharp precision.

Yes. It could be so very simple. The thought made me sick, but the possibility of losing Olivia all over again was far worse.

She came before anyone and anything. That was all there was to it.

"All right," I said with feigned resignation. "You found me. I'm not really set up for entertaining here. Why don't I come to you?"

When I got off the phone, I went to the bottom of the stairs and called up to Bash. He appeared in an instant, his expression taut.

"The shrouded folk have her," I said simply. "I'm going to bring her back. But to make sure I actually get to do that, we need to accomplish one thing first."

"What exactly is it you wanted to show me up here?" Sherlock said, peering across the mountain slope.

I nudged him onward along the narrow rocky path. Our shoes rasped against the stone. "It's just a little farther. I'm not entirely sure what to make of it. It's difficult to explain without you seeing it."

"But you didn't want John and Garrett making their own observations?"

"They can come take a look later if you think it's a good idea. For now I'd like your perceptions only, without any distractions."

An appeal to ego always smoothed over a request with Sherlock. I could tell he didn't believe I'd told him the whole story, but he'd gone along with my somewhat strange invitation to see where it led anyway.

Because he didn't believe it could lead anywhere all that awful. Because he trusted that my intentions were good even when I was dissembling. That was going to be his biggest mistake.

I resisted the urge to ball my hands and strode on toward the spot I'd identified yesterday. The mountainside fell away with a nearly sheer drop at our right, gray scree spotted with tufts of grass and weeds.

It felt as if we'd left summer behind this high up. The wind whipped past me with a chilling bite. I didn't let myself shiver.

Bash was off doing his part. I'd timed the walk as he and I had discussed. If I looked back the way we'd come, if I peered for the vehicle and the figures that should be emerging from it right now, Sherlock would definitely notice that. I couldn't afford to give the game away, so I kept my gaze trained on the path ahead. On the man ahead of me who I admired so much my chest stung with it right now.

I couldn't think about the passion I'd woken in him and how delighted he'd been to provoke as much pleasure in me. I couldn't think about the thrill of matching wits with him time and time again. None of that matter. Not when Olivia was waiting for me.

My pulse was thumping hard and heavy. I kept my posture straight even though it wanted to hunch against the awful task I was about to complete.

This was necessary. It was all necessary, from the act itself to Bash bringing John and Garrett as distant witnesses. After all this time when she must have thought I'd abandoned her, I owed it to Olivia to give her everything I could.

Even if it meant sacrificing everything new and wonderful I'd discovered in myself in the last few months.

We'd reached the spot. I knew from the knob of rock that jutted from the ground beside the path. I stopped and pointed toward an imaginary object down the slope. "There. Can you see it? It's small, so it's hard to make out."

Sherlock frowned and eased closer to the edge. I watched his feet, his stance. He bent over to peer in the direction I'd pointed. "Can you give me a better idea what you're looking at?"

A way out. A severing as utter as the one that sliced my sister's toe from her foot.

One last thread of resistance trembled through me. I gritted my teeth against it. Then I smacked my hand into Sherlock's back and shoved as hard as I could down the sheer treacherous drop.

Eva Chase lives in Canada with her family. She loves stories both swoony and supernatural, and strong women and the men who appreciate them. Along with the Moriarty's Men series, she is the author of the Looking Glass Curse trilogy, the Their Dark Valkyrie series, the Witch's Consorts series, the Dragon Shifter's Mates series, the Demons of Fame Romance series, the Legends Reborn trilogy, and the Alpha Project Psychic Romance series.

Connect with Eva online:
www.evachase.com
eva@evachase.com